William Black

White Heather

Vol. III

William Black

White Heather
Vol. III

ISBN/EAN: 9783743395145

Manufactured in Europe, USA, Canada, Australia, Japa

Cover: Foto ©Andreas Hilbeck / pixelio.de

Manufactured and distributed by brebook publishing software (www.brebook.com)

William Black

White Heather

WHITE HEATHER

A Novel

BY

WILLIAM BLACK

AUTHOR OF 'MACLEOD OF DARE,' 'JUDITH SHAKESPEARE,' ETC.

IN THREE VOLUMES

VOL. III.

London

MACMILLAN AND CO.

1885

CONTENTS OF VOL. III.

CHAPTER XIII.

CHAPTER XIV.

CHAPTER XV.

CHAPTER XVI.

WHITE HEATHER.

CHAPTER I.

A MESSAGE.

CLEAR and brilliant in their blue and white are these shining northern skies; and the winds that come blowing over the moorland are honey-scented from the heather; and the wide waters of the loch are all of a ruffled and shimmering silver, with a thin fringe of foam along the curving bays. And this is Love Meenie that comes out from the cottage and comes down to the road; with perhaps less of the wild-rose tint in her cheeks than used to be there, and less of the ready light of gladness that used to leap into her blue-gray eyes; but still with that constant gentleness of expression that seems to bring her into accord with all the beautiful things in the landscape around her. And, indeed, on this particular morning she is cheerful enough; walking briskly, chatting to the ancient terrier that is trotting at her side, and equably regarding now the velvet-soft shadows that steal along the sunlit slopes of Clebrig. and now the wheeling and circling of some peewits that have been startled from their marshy haunts by the side of the stream.

'And who knows but that there may be a message or a

bit of news for us this morning?' she says to the faithful
Harry. 'For yonder comes the mail. And indeed it's
well for you, my good little chap, that you can't understand
how far away Glasgow is; I suppose you expect to see your
master at any minute, at every turn of the road. And if
he should send you a message—or Maggie either—how am
I to tell you?'

The pretty Nelly is at the door of the inn, scattering
food to the fowls.

'It's a peautiful moarning, Miss Douglas,' she says.

And here is Mr. Murray, with his pipe, and his occultly
humorous air.

'And are you come along for your letters, Miss Meenie?'
he says. 'Ay, ay, it is not an unusual thing for a young
leddy to be anxious about a letter—it is not an unusual
thing at ahl.'

And now the mail-car comes swinging up to the door;
the one or two passengers alight, glad to stretch their legs;
the letter bags are hauled down, and Miss Douglas follows
them indoors. Mrs. Murray, who acts as post-mistress, is
not long in sorting out the contents.

'Two for me?' says Meenie. 'And both from Glasgow?
Well, now, that does not often happen.'

But of course she could not further interrupt the post-
mistress in the performance of her duties; so she put the
letters in her pocket; passed out from the inn and through
the little crowd of loiterers; and made for the high-road
and for home. She was in no hurry to open these budgets
of news. Such things came but once in a while to this
remote hamlet; and when they did come they were leisurely
and thoroughly perused—not skimmed and thrown aside.
Nevertheless when she got up to the high-road she thought

she would pause there for just a second, and run her eye over the pages, lest there might be some mention of Ronald's name. She had heard of him but little of late; and he had never once written to her—perhaps he had no excuse for doing so. It was through Maggie that from time to time she got news of him; and now it was Maggie's letter that she opened first.

Well, there was not much about Ronald. Maggie was at school; Ronald was busy; he seldom came over to the minister's house. And so Meenie, with a bit of a sigh, put that letter into her pocket, and turned to the other. But now she was indifferent and careless. It was not likely that her sister had anything to say about Ronald; for he had not yet called at the house. Moreover, Mrs. Gemmill, from two or three expressions she had used, did not seem anxious to make his acquaintance.

And then the girl's breath caught, and she became suddenly pale. '*Drinking himself to death, in the lowest of low company*'—these were the words confronting her startled eyes; and the next instant she had darted a glance along the road, and another back towards the inn, as if with a sudden strange fear that some one had overseen. No, she was all alone; with the quickly closed letter in her trembling hand; her brain bewildered; her heart beating; and with a kind of terror on her face. And then, rather blindly, she turned and walked away in the other direction —not towards her own home; and still held the letter tightly clasped, as if she feared that some one might get at this ghastly secret.

'*Ronald!—Ronald!*'—there was a cry of anguish in her heart; for this was all too sharp and sudden an end to certain wistful dreams and fancies. These were the dreams

and fancies of long wakeful nights, when she would lie and
wonder what was the meaning of his farewell look towards
her; and wonder if he could guess that his going away was
to change all her life for her; and wonder whether, if all
things were to go well with him, he would come back and
claim her love—that was there awaiting him, and would
always await him, whether he ever came back or no.   And
sometimes, indeed, the morning light brought a joyous
assurance with it; she knew well why he had not ventured
to hand her that tell-tale message that he had actually
written out and addressed to her; but in the glad future,
when he could come with greater confidence and declare
the truth—would she allow father, or mother, or any one
else to interfere?   On these mornings the Mudal-Water
seemed to laugh as it went rippling by; it had a friendly
sound; she could hear it

*' Move the sweet forget-me-nots
That grow for happy lovers.'*

And at such times her favourite and secret reading was of
women who had been bold and generous with their love;
and she feared she had been timid and had fallen in too
easily with her mother's schemes for her; but now that she
understood herself better—now that her heart had revealed
itself plainly to her—surely, if ever that glad time were to
come—if ever she were to see him hasten along to the little
garden-gate—on the very first moment of his arrival—she
would not stint her welcome of him?   White, white were
the mornings on which such fancies filled her head; and
the Mudal laughed along its clear brown shallows; and
there was a kind of music in the moorland air.

' Drinking himself to death, in the lowest of low company.'

black night seemed to have fallen upon her, and a wild bewilderment, and a crushing sense of hopelessness that shut out for ever those fair visions of the future. She did not stay to ask whether this might not be a woman's exaggeration or the mere gossip of a straitlaced set; the blow had fallen too suddenly to let her reason about it; she only knew that the very pride of her life, the secret hope of her heart, had been in a moment extinguished. And Ronald— Ronald that was ever the smartest and handsomest of them all—the gayest and most audacious, the very king of all the company whithersoever he went—was it this same Ronald who had in so short a time become a bleared and besotted drunkard, shunning the public ways, hiding in ignoble haunts, with the basest of creatures for his only friends? And she—that had been so proud of him—that had been so assured of his future—nay, that had given him the love of her life, and had sworn to herself that, whether he ever came to claim it or no, no other man should take his place in her heart—she it was who had become possessed of this dreadful secret, while all the others were still imagining that Ronald was as the Ronald of yore. She dared not go back to Inver-Mudal—not yet, at least. She went away along the highway; and then left that for a path that led alongside a small burn; and by and by, when she came to a place where she was screened from all observation by steep and wooded banks, she sat down there with some kind of vague notion that she ought more carefully to read this terrible news; but presently she had flung herself, face downward, on the heather, in an utter agony of grief, and there she lay and sobbed and cried, with her head buried in her hands. '*Ronald! Ronald!*' her heart seemed to call aloud in its despair; but how was any appeal to be

carried to him—away to Glasgow town? And was this the
end? Was he never coming back? The proud young life
that promised so fair to be sucked under and whirled away
in a black current; and as for her—for her the memory of
a few happy days spent on Mudal's banks, and years and
years of lonely thinking over what might have been.

A sharp whistle startled her; and she sprang to her feet,
and hastily dried her eyes. A Gordon setter came ranging
through the strip of birch-wood, and then its companion;
both dogs merely glanced at her—they were far too intent
on their immediate work to take further notice. And then
it quickly occurred to her that, if this were Lord Ailine
who was coming along, perhaps she might appeal to him
—she might beg of him to write to Ronald—or even to
go to Glasgow—for had not these two been companions
and friends? And he was a man—he would know what
to do—what could she do, a helpless girl? Presently
Lord Ailine appeared, coming leisurely along the banks
of the little stream in company with a keeper and a
young lad; and when he saw her, he raised his cap and
greeted her.

'Don't let us disturb you, Miss Douglas,' said he.
'Gathering flowers for the dinner-table, I suppose?'

'I hope I have done no harm,' said she, though her
mind was so agitated that she scarcely knew what she said.
'I—I have not seen any birds—nor a hare either.'

'Harm? No, no,' he said good-naturedly. 'I hope
your mamma is quite well. There's a haunch of a roe-
buck at the lodge that Duncan can take along this afternoon——'

'Your lordship,' said the keeper reprovingly, 'there's
Bella drawing on to something.'

'Good morning, Miss Douglas,' he said quickly, and the next moment he was off.

But even during that brief interview she had instinctively arrived at the conclusion that it was not for her to spread about this bruit in Inver-Mudal. She could not. This news about Ronald to come from her lips—with perhaps this or that keeper to carry it on to the inn and make it the topic of general wonder there? They would hear of it soon enough. But no one—not even any one in her own household—would be able to guess what it meant to her; as yet she herself could hardly realise it, except that all of a sudden her life seemed to have grown dark.

She had to get back to the cottage in time for the mid-day dinner, and she sate at table there, pale and silent, and with a consciousness as of guilt weighing upon her. She even did her best to eat something, in order to avoid their remarks and looks; but she failed in that, and was glad to get away as soon as she could to the privacy of her own room.

'I'm sure I don't know what's the matter with William-ina,' Mrs. Douglas said with a sigh. 'She has not been looking herself for many a day back; and she seems going from bad to worse—she ate hardly a scrap at dinner.'

Of course it was for the Doctor to prescribe.

'She wants a change,' he said.

'A change,' the little dame retorted with some asperity, for this was a sore subject with her. 'She would have had a change long before now, but for her and you together. Three months ago I wanted her sent to Glasgow——'

'Glasgow—for any one in indifferent health—' the big bland Doctor managed to interpolate; but she would not listen.

'I'm sure I don't understand the girl. She has no proper pride. Any other girl in her position would be glad to have such chances, and eager to make use of them. But no—she would sooner go looking after a lot of cottar's children than set to work to qualify herself for taking her proper place in society; and what is the use of my talking when you encourage her in her idleness?'

'I like to have the girl at home,' he said, rather feebly.

'There,' she said, producing a letter and opening it—although he had heard the contents a dozen times before. 'There it is—in black and white—a distinct invitation. "Could you let Meenie come to us for a month or six weeks when we go to Brighton in November?"'

'Well,' said the good-natured Doctor, 'that would be a better kind of a change. Sea-air—sunlight—plenty of society and amusement.'

'She shall not go there, nor anywhere else, with my cousin and his family, until she has fitted herself for taking such a position,' said the little woman peremptorily. 'Sir Alexander is good-nature itself, but I am not going to send him a half-educated Highland girl that he would be ashamed of. Why, the best families in England go to Brighton for the winter—every one is there. It would be worse than sending her to London. And what does this month or six weeks mean?—Surely it is plain enough. They want to try her. They want to see what her accomplishments are. They want to see whether they can take her abroad with them, and present her at Paris and Florence and Rome. Every year now Sir Alexander goes abroad at Christmas time; and of course if she satisfied them she would be asked to go also—and there, think of that chance!'

' The girl is well enough,' said he.

She was on the point of retorting that, as far as he knew anything about the matter, Williamina was well enough. But she spared him.

' No, she has no proper pride,' the little Dresden-china woman continued. ' And just now, when everything is in her favour. Agatha never had such chances. Agatha never had Williamina's good looks. Of course, I say nothing against Mr. Gemmill—he is a highly respectable man —and if the business is going on as they say it is going, I don't see why they should not leave Queen's Crescent and take a larger house—up by the West End Park. And he is an intelligent man, too; the society they have is clever and intellectual—you saw in Agatha's last letter about the artists' party she had—why, their names are in every newspaper—quite distinguished people, in that way of life. And, at all events, it would be a beginning. Williamina would learn something. Agatha is a perfect musician—you can't deny that.'

But here the big Doctor rebelled; and he brought the weight of his professional authority to bear upon her.

' Now, look here, Jane, when I said that the girl wanted a change, I meant a change; but not a change to singing-lessons, and music-lessons, and German lessons, and Italian lessons, and not a change to an atmosphere like that of Glasgow. Bless my soul, do you think *that* kind of change will bring back the colour to her cheek, and give her an appetite, and put some kind of cheerfulness into her? Queen's Crescent! She's not going to Queen's Crescent with my will. Brighton, if you like.'

' Brighton? To get herself laughed at, and put in the background, as a half-educated ignorant Highland peasant girl? So long as she is what she is, she shall not go to Brighton with my will.'

So here was an absolute dead-lock so far as Meenie's future was concerned; but she knew nothing of it; and if she had known she would not have heeded much. It was not of her own future she was thinking. And it seemed so terrible to her to know that there was nothing she would not have adventured to save this man from destruction, and to know that she was incapable of doing anything at all. If she could but see him for a moment—to make an appeal to him; if she could but take his hand in hers; would she not say that there had been timidity, doubt, misapprehension in the past, but that now there was no time for any of these; she had come to claim him and save him and restore him to himself—no matter what he might think of her? Indeed she tried to put all thought of herself out of the matter. She would allow no self-pride to interfere, if only she could be of the smallest aid to him, if she could stretch out her hand to him, and appeal to him, and drag him back. But how? She seemed so helpless. And yet her anxiety drove her to the consideration of a hundred wild and impossible schemes, insomuch that she could not rest in her own room, to which she had retreated for safety and quiet. She put on her bonnet again and went out—still with that guilty consciousness of a secret hanging over her; and she went down the road and over the bridge; and then away up the solitary valley through which the Mudal flows. Alas! there was no laughing over the brown shallows now; there was no thinking of

> *' the sweet forget-me-nots,*
> *That grow for happy lovers ';*

all had become dark around her; and the giant grasp of

Glasgow had taken him away from her, and dragged him down, and blotted out for ever the visions of a not impossible future with which she had been wont to beguile the solitary hours. '*Drinking himself to death, in the lowest of low company :*' could this be Ronald, that but a few months ago had been the gayest of any, with audacious talk of what he was going to try for, with health and happiness radiant in his eyes? And it seemed to her that her sister Agatha had been proud of writing these words, and proud of the underlining of them, and that there was a kind of vengeance in them; and the girl's mouth was shut hard; and she was making vague and fierce resolutions of showing to all of them—far and near—that she was not ashamed of her regard for Ronald Strang, gamekeeper or no gamekeeper, if ever the chance should serve. Ashamed! He had been for her the very king of men—in his generosity, his courage, his gentleness, his manliness, his modesty, and his staunch and unfaltering fealty to his friends. And was he to fall away from that ideal, and to become a wreck, a waif, an outcast; and she to stand by and not stretch out a hand to save?

But what could she do? All the day she pondered; all the evening; and through the long, silent, and wakeful night. And when, at last, as the gray of the dawn showed in the small window, she had selected one of these hundred bewildered plans and schemes, it seemed a fantastic thing that she was about to do. She would send him a piece of white heather. He would know it came from her—he would recognise the postmark, and also her handwriting. And if he took it as a message and an appeal, as a token of good wishes and friendliness, and the hope of better fortune? Or if—and here she fell a-trembling, for it was

a little cold in these early hours—if he should take it as
a confession, as an unmaidenly declaration? Oh, she did
not care. It was all she could think of doing; and do
something she must. And she remembered with a timid
and nervous joy her own acknowledged influence over him
—had not Maggie talked of it a thousand times?—and if
he were to recognise this message in its true light, what
then? '*Ronald! Ronald!*' her heart was still calling, with
something of a tremulous hope amid all its grief and pity.

She was out and abroad over the moorland long before any
one was astir, and searching with an anxious diligence, and
as yet without success. White heather is not so frequently
met with in the North as in the West Highlands; and yet in
Sutherlandshire it is not an absolute rarity; many a time
had she come across a little tuft of it in her wanderings
over the moors. But now, search as she might, she could
not find the smallest bit; and time began to press; for this
was the morning for the mail to go south—if she missed it,
she would have to wait two more days. And as half-hour
after half-hour went by, she became more anxious and
nervous and agitated; she went rapidly from knoll to knoll,
seeking the likeliest places; and all in vain. It was a question of minutes now. She could hear the mail-cart on the
road behind her; soon it would pass her and go on to the
inn, where it would remain but a brief while before setting
out again for Lairg. And presently, when the mail-cart
did come along and go by, then she gave up the quest in
despair; and in a kind of bewildered way set out for home.
Her heart was heavy and full of its disappointment; and
her face was paler a little than usual; but at least her eyes
told no tales.

And then, all of a sudden, as she was crossing the Mudal

bridge, she caught sight of a little tuft of gray away along the bank and not far from the edge of the stream. At first she thought it was merely a patch of withered heather; and then a wild hope possessed her; she quickly left the bridge and made her way towards it; and the next moment she was joyfully down on her knees, selecting the whitest spray she could find. And the mail-cart?—it would still be at the inn—the inn was little more than half a mile off—could she run hard and intercept them after all, and send her white-dove message away to the south? To think of it was to try it, at all events; and she ran as no town-bred girl ever ran in her life—past the Doctor's cottage, along the wide and empty road, past the keeper's house and the kennels, across the bridge that spans the little burn. Alas! there was the mail-cart already on its way.

'Johnnie, Johnnie!' she called.

Happily the wind was blowing towards him; he heard, looked back, and pulled up his horses.

'Wait a minute—I have a letter for you to take!' she called, though her strength was all gone now.

And yet she managed to get quickly down to the inn, and astonished Mrs. Murray by breathlessly begging for an envelope.

'Tell Nelly—tell Nelly,' she said, while her trembling fingers wrote the address, 'to come and take this to the mail-cart—they're waiting—Johnnie will post it at Lairg.'

And then, when she had finished the tremulous address, and carefully dried it with the blotting-paper, and given the little package to Nelly, and bade her run—quick, quick—to hand it to the driver, then the girl sank back in the chair and began laughing in a strange, half-hysterical way, and then that became a burst of crying, with her face hidden in her hands. But the good-hearted Mrs. Murray was there; and her arms were round the girl's neck; and she was saying, in her gentle Highland way—

'Well, well, now, to think you should hef had such a run to catch the mail-cart—and no wonder you are dead-beat—ay, ay, and you not looking so well of late, Miss Meenie. But you will just rest here a while; and Nelly will get you some tea; and there is no need for you to go back home until you have come to yourself better. No, you hef not been looking well lately; and you must not tire yourself like this—dear me, the place would be quite different alhtogether if anything was to make you ill.'

CHAPTER II.

IT was as late as half-past ten o'clock—and on a sufficiently gray and dull and cheerless morning—that Ronald's landlady, surprised not to have heard him stirring, knocked at his room. There was no answer. Then she knocked again, opened the door an inch or two, and dropped a letter on the floor.

'Are ye no up yet?'

The sound of her voice aroused him.

'In a minute, woman,' he said sleepily; and, being thus satisfied, the landlady went off, shutting the door behind her.

He rose in the bed and looked around him, in a dazed fashion. He was already partially dressed, for he had been up two hours before, but had thrown himself down on the bed again, over-fatigued, half-stupefied, and altogether discontented. The fact is, he had come home the night before in a reckless mood, and had sate on through hour after hour until it was nearly dawn, harassing himself with idle dreams and idle regrets, drinking to drown care, smoking incessantly, sometimes scrawling half-scornful rhymes. There were all the evidences now on the table before him—a whisky-bottle, a tumbler, a wooden pipe and plenty of ashes, a sheet of paper scrawled over in an un-

certain hand.   He took up that sheet to recall what he had
written :

> *King Death came striding along the road,*
> *And he laughed aloud to see*
> *How every rich man's mother's son*
> *Would take to his heels and flee.*
>
> *Duke, lord, or merchant, off they skipped,*
> *Whenever that he drew near ;*
> *And they dropped their guineas as wild they ran,*
> *And their faces were white with fear.*
>
> *But the poor folk labouring in the fields*
> *Watched him as he passed by ;*
> *And they took to their spades and mattocks again,*
> *And turned to their work with a sigh.*
>
> *Then farther along the road he saw*
> *An old man sitting alone ;*
> *His head lay heavy upon his hands,*
> *And sorrowful was his moan.*
>
> *Old age had shrivelled and bent his frame ;*
> *Age and hard work together*
> *Had scattered his locks, and bleared his eyes—*
> *Age and the winter weather.*
>
> *'Old man,' said Death, 'do you tremble to know*
> *That now you are near the end ?'*
> *The old man looked : 'You are Death,' said he,*
> *'And at last I've found a friend.'*

It was a strange kind of mood for a young fellow to
have fallen into ; but he did not seem to think so.   As he
contemplated the scrawled lines—with rather an absent
and preoccupied air—this was what he was saying to
himself—

'If the old gentleman would only come striding along
the Port Dundas Road, I know one that would be glad

enough to go out and meet him and shake hands with him, this very minute.'

He went to the window and threw it open, and sate down : the outer air would be pleasanter than this inner atmosphere, impregnated with the fumes of whisky and tobacco ; and his head was burning, and his pulses heavy. But the dreariness of this outlook !—the gray pavements, the gray railway station, the gray sheds, the gray skies ; and evermore the dull slumberous sound of the great city already plunged in its multitudinous daily toil. Then he began to recall the events of the preceding evening ; and had not Mrs. Menzies promised to call for him, about eleven, to drive him out to see some of her acquaintances at Miln- gavie ? Well, it would be something to do ; it would be a relief to get into the fresher air—to get away from this hopeless and melancholy neighbourhood. Kate Menzies had high spirits ; she could laugh away remorse and discontent and depression ; she could make the hours go by somehow. And now, as it was almost eleven, he would finish his dressing and be ready to set out when she called ; as for breakfast, no thought of that entered his mind.

Then he chanced to see something white lying on the floor—an envelope—perhaps this was a note from Kate, saying she was too busy that morning and could not come for him ? He went and took up the letter ; and instantly —as he regarded the address on it—a kind of bewilder- ment, almost of fear, appeared on his face. For well he knew Meenie's handwriting : had he not pondered over every characteristic of it—the precise small neatness of it, the long loops of the *l*'s, the German look of the capital R ? And why should Meenie write to him ?

He opened the envelope and took out the bit of white heather that Meenie had so hastily despatched : there was no message, not the smallest scrap of writing. But was not this a message—and full of import, too; for surely Meenie would not have adopted this means of communicating with him at the mere instigation of an idle fancy? And why should she have sent it—and at this moment? Had she heard, then? Had any gossip about him reached Inver-Mudal? And how much had she heard? There was a kind of terror in his heart as he went slowly back to the window, and sate down there, still staring absently at this token that had been sent him, and trying hard to make out the meaning of it. What was in Meenie's mind? What was her intention? Not merely to give him a sprig of white heather with wishes for good luck; there was more than that, as he easily guessed; but how much more? And at first there was little of joy or gladness or gratitude in his thinking; there was rather fear, and a wondering as to what Meenie had heard of him, and a sickening sense of shame. The white gentleness of the message did not strike him; it was rather a reproach—a recalling of other days—Meenie's eyes were regarding him with proud indignation—this was all she had to say to him now.

A man's voice was heard outside; the door was brusquely opened; Jimmy Laidlaw appeared.

'What, man, no ready yet? Are ye just out o' your bed? Where's your breakfast? Dinna ye ken it's eleven o'clock?'

Ronald regarded him with no friendly eye. He wished to be alone; there was much to think of; there was more in his mind than the prospect of a rattling, devil-may-care drive out to Milngavie.

'Is Kate below?' said he.

'She is that. Look sharp, man, and get on your coat. She doesna like to keep the cob standing.'

'Look here, Laidlaw,' Ronald said, 'I wish ye would do me a good turn. Tell her that—that I'll be obliged if she will excuse me ; I'm no up to the mark ; ye'll have a merrier time of it if ye go by yourselves ; there now, like a good fellow, make it straight wi' her.'

'Do ye want her to jump doon ma throat?' retorted Mr. Laidlaw, with a laugh. 'I'll tak' no sic message. Come, come, man, pull yoursel' thegither. What's the matter? Hammer and tongs in your head?—the fresh air 'll drive that away. Come along !'

'The last word's the shortest,' Ronald said stubbornly. 'I'm not going. Tell her not to take it ill—I'm—I'm obliged to her, tell her——'

'Indeed, I'll leave you and her to fight it out between ye,' said Laidlaw. 'D'ye think I want the woman to snap my head off?'

He left, and Ronald fondly hoped that they would drive away and leave him to himself. But presently there was a light tapping at the door.

'Ronald !'

He recognised the voice, and he managed to throw a coat over his shoulders—just as Kate Menzies, without further ceremony, made her appearance.

'What's this now?' exclaimed the buxom widow—who was as radiant and good-natured and smartly dressed as ever—'what does this daft fellow Laidlaw mean by bringing me a message like that? I ken ye better, Ronald, my lad. Down in the mouth?—take a hair o' the dog that bit ye. Here, see, I'll pour it out for ye.'

She went straight to the bottle, uncorked it, and poured out about a third of a tumblerful of whisky.

'Ronald, Ronald, ye're an ill lad to want this in the morning; but what must be, must; here, put some life into ye. The day'll be just splendid outside the town; and old Jaap's with us too; and I've got a hamper; and somewhere or other we'll camp out, like a band of gypsies. Dinna fear, lad; I'll no drag ye into the MacDougals' house until we're on the way back; and then it'll just be a cup o' tea and a look at the bairns, and on we drive again to the town. What's the matter? Come on, my lad!— we'll have a try at "Cauld Kail in Aberdeen" when we get away frae the houses.'

'Katie, lass,' said he, rather shamefacedly, 'I'm—I'm sorry that I promised—but I'll take it kind of ye to excuse me—I'm no in the humour someway—and ye'll be better by yourselves——'

'Ay, and what good 'll ye do by pu'ing a wry mouth?' said she tauntingly. '"The devil was ill, the devil a saint would be." Here, man! it's no the best medicine, but it's better than none.'

She took the whisky to him, and gave him a hearty slap on the shoulder. There was a gleam of sullen fire in his eye.

'It's ill done of ye, woman, to drive a man against his will,' he said, and he retreated from her a step or two.

'Oh,' said she proudly, and she threw the whisky into the coal-scuttle, and slammed the tumbler down on the table, for she had a temper too, 'if ye'll no be coaxed, there's them that will. If that's what Long John does for your temper, I'd advise you to change and try Talisker. Good morning to ye, my braw lad, and thank ye for your courtesy.'

She stalked from the room, and banged the door behind

her when she left. But she was really a good-hearted kind
of creature; before she had reached the outer door she
had recovered herself; and she turned and came into the
room again, a single step or so.

'Ronald,' she said, in quite a different voice, 'it 'll no
be for your good to quarrel wi' me——'

'I wish for no quarrel wi' ye, Katie, woman——'

'For I look better after ye than some o' them. If ye'll
no come for the drive, will ye look in in the afternoon or
at night, if it suits ye better? Seven o'clock, say—to show
that there's no ill feeling between us.'

'Yes, I will,' said he—mainly to get rid of her; for,
indeed, he could scarcely hear what she was saying to him
for thinking of this strange and mysterious message that
had come to him from Meenie.

And then, when she had gone, he rapidly washed and
dressed, and went away out from the house—out by the
Cowcaddens, and Shamrock Street, and West Prince's
Street, and over the Kelvin, and up to Hillhead, to certain
solitary thoroughfares he had discovered in his devious
wanderings; and all the time he was busy with various
interpretations of this message from Meenie and of her
reasons for sending it. At first, as has been said, there
was nothing for him but shame and self-abasement; this
was a reproach; she had heard of the condition into which
he had fallen; this was to remind him of what had been.
And indeed, it was now for the first time that he began to
be conscious of what that condition was. He had fled to
those boon-companions as a kind of refuge from the hopelessness of the weary hours, from the despair with regard to
the future that had settled down over his life. He had laughed,
drunk, smoked, and sung the time away, glad to forget. When

haunting memories came to rebuke, then there was a call
for another glass, another song. Nay, he could even make
apologies to himself when the immediate excitement was
over. Why should he do otherwise? The dreams conjured up
by the Americans had no more charms for him. Why should
he work towards some future that had no interest for him?

> *Death is the end of life ; ah, why*
> *Should life all labour be ?*

And so Kate Menzies's dog-cart became a pleasant thing, as
it rattled along the hard stony roads ; and many a merry
glass they had at the wayside inns ; and then home again
in the evening to supper, and singing, and a good-night
bacchanalian festival at the Harmony Club. The hours
passed ; he did not wish to think of what his life had become ; enough if, for the time being, he could banish the
horrors of the aching head, the hot pulse, the trembling hands.

But if Meenie had heard of all this, how would it appear
to her? and he made no doubt that she had heard. It
was some powerful motive that had prompted her to do this
thing. He knew that her sister had been making inquiries
about him ; his brother's congregation was a hot-bed of
gossip ; if any news of him had been sent by that agency,
no doubt it was the worst. And still Meenie did not turn
away from him with a shudder? He took out the envelope
again. What could she mean? Might he dare to think it
was this—that, no matter what had happened, or what she
had heard, she still had some little faith in him, that the recollection of their old friendship was not all gone away? Reproach it might be—but perhaps also an appeal? And if
Meenie had still some interest in what happened to him——?

He would go no farther than that. It was characteristic
of the man that, even with this white token of goodwill and

remembrance and good wishes before his eyes—with this unusual message just sent to him from one who was generally so shy and reserved—he permitted to himself no wildly daring fancies or bewildering hopes. Nor had the majesty of the Stuarts of Glengask and Orosay anything to do with this restraint : it was the respect that he paid to Meenie herself. And yet—and yet this was a friendly token; it seemed to make the day whiter somehow; it was with no ill-will she had been thinking of him when she gathered it from one of the knolls at the foot of Clebrig or from the banks of Mudal-Water. So white and fresh it was; it spoke of clear skies and sweet moorland winds: and there seemed to be the soft touch of her fingers still on it as she had pressed it into the envelope; and it was Meenie's own small white hand that had written that rather trembling '*Mr. Ronald Strang.*' A gentle message ; he grew to think that there was less of reproach in it; if she had heard evil tidings of him, perhaps she was sorry more than anything else ; Meenie's eyes might have sorrow in them and pain, but anger—never. And her heart— well, surely her heart could not have been set bitterly against him, or she would not have sent him this mute little token of remembrance, as if to recall the olden days.

And then he rose and drove against the bars that caged him in. Why should the ghastly farce be played any longer ? Why should he go through that dull mechanical routine in which he had no interest whatever ? Let others make what money they choose ; let others push forward to any future that they might think desirable : let them aim at being first in the world's fight for wealth, and having saloon-carriages, and steam-yachts on Lake Michigan, and cat-boats on Lake George : but as for him, if Lord Ailine,

now, would only let him go back to the little hamlet in the
northern wilds, and give him charge of the dogs again, and
freedom to ask Dr. Douglas to go with him for a turn at
the mountain hares or for a day's salmon-fishing on the
Mudal—in short, if only he could get back to his old life
again, with fair skies over him, and fresh blowing winds
around him, and wholesome blood running cheerily through
his veins?   And then the chance, at some hour or other of
the long day, of meeting Meenie, and finding the beautiful,
timid, Highland eyes fixed on his : 'Are you going along
to the inn, Ronald?' he could almost hear her say.   'And
will you be so kind as to take these letters for me?'

But contracted habits are not so easily shaken off as all
that ; and he was sick and ill at ease ; and when the hour
came for him to go down and see Kate Menzies and her
friends, perhaps he was not altogether sorry that he had
made a definite promise which he was bound to keep.   He
left the envelope, with its piece of white heather, at home.

Nevertheless, he was rather dull, they thought ; and
there was some facetious raillery over his not having yet recovered from the frolic of the previous night ; with frequent
invitations to take a hair of the dog that had bitten him.
Kate was the kindest ; she had been a little alarmed by the
definite repugnance he had shown in the morning ; she was
glad to be friends with him again.   As for him—well, he
was as good-natured as ever ; but rather absent in manner ;
for sometimes, amid all their boisterous *camaraderie*, he
absolutely forgot what they were saying; and in a kind of
dream he seemed to see before him the sunlit Strath-Terry,
and the blue waters of the loch, and Mudal's stream wind-
ing through the solitary moorland waste—and a young girl
there stooping to pick up something from the heather.

CHAPTER III.

A RESOLVE.

THE days passed; no answer came to that mute message of hers; nay, how could she expect any answer? But these were terrible days to her—of mental torture, and heart-searching, and unceasing and unsatisfied longing, and yearning, and pity. And then out of all this confusion of thinking and suffering there gradually grew up a clear and definite resolve. What if she were to make of that bit of white heather but an *avant-courier?* What if she were herself to go to Glasgow, and seek him out, and confront him, and take him by the hand? She had not overrated her old influence with him : well she knew that. And how could she stand by idle and allow him to perish? The token she had sent him must have told him of her thinking of him; he would be prepared; perhaps he would even guess that she had come to Glasgow for his sake? Well, she did not mind that much; Ronald would have gentle thoughts of her, whatever happened; and this need was far too sore and pressing to permit of timid and sensitive hesitations.

One morning she went to her father's room and tapped at the door.

'Come in !'

She was rather pale as she entered.

'Father,' she said, 'I would like to go to Glasgow for a while.'

Her father turned in his chair and regarded her.

'What's the matter with ye, my girl?' he said. 'You've not been looking yourself at all for some time back, and these last few days you've practically eaten nothing. And yet your mother declares there's nothing the matter. Glasgow? I dare say a change would do you good— cheer you up a bit, and that; but—Glasgow? More schooling, more fees, that would be the chief result, I imagine; and that's what your mother's driving at. I think it's nonsense: you're a grown woman; you've learned everything that will ever be of any use to you.'

'I ought to have, any way, by this time,' Meenie said simply. 'And indeed it is not for that, father. I—I should like to go to Glasgow for a while.'

'There's Lady Stuart would have ye stay with them at Brighton for a few weeks; but your mother seems to think you should go amongst them as a kind of Mezzofanti—it's precious little of that there's about Sir Alexander, as I know well. However, if you're not to go to them until you are polished out of all human shape and likeness, I suppose I must say nothing——'

'But I would rather go and stay with Agatha, father,' the girl said.

He looked at her again.

'Well,' said he, 'I do think something must be done. It would be a fine thing for you—you of all creatures in the world—to sink into a hopeless anæmic condition. Lassie, where's that eldritch laugh o' yours gone to? And I see you go dawdling along the road—you that could beat a young roedeer if you were to try. Glasgow?—well, I'll see what your mother says.'

'Thank you, father,' she said, but she did not leave at once. 'I think I heard you say that Mr. Blair was going south on Monday,' she timidly suggested.

This Mr. Blair was a U.P. minister from Glasgow, who was taking a well-earned holiday up at Tongue—fishing in the various lochs in that neighbourhood—and who was known to the Douglases.

'You're in a deuce of a hurry, Miss,' her father said, but good-naturedly enough. 'You mean you could go to Glasgow under his escort?'

'Yes.'

'Well, I will see what your mother says—I suppose she will be for making a fuss over the necessary preparations.'

But this promise and half permission had instantly brought to the girl a kind of frail and wandering joy and hope; and there was a brief smile on her face as she said—

'Well, you know, father, if I have to get any things I ought to get them in Glasgow. The preparations at Inver-Mudal can't take much time.'

'I will see what your mother thinks about it,' said the big, good-humoured Doctor, who was cautious about assenting to anything until the ruler and lawgiver of the house had been consulted.

The time was short, but the chance of sending Meenie to Glasgow under charge of the Rev. Mr. Blair was opportune; and Mrs. Douglas had no scruple about making use of this temporary concern on the part of her husband about Meenie's health for the working out of her own ends. Of course the girl was only going away to be

brightened up by a little society. The change of air
might possibly do her good. There could be no doubt
she had been looking ill; and in her sister's house she
would have every attention paid her, quite as much as if
she were in her own home. All the same, Mrs. Douglas
was resolved that this opportunity for finally fitting Meenie
for that sphere in which she hoped to see her move should
not be lost. Agatha should have private instructions.
And Agatha herself was a skilled musician. Moreover,
some little society—of a kind—met at Mr. Gemmill's
house; the time would not be entirely lost, even if a little
economy in the matter of fees was practised, in deference
to the prejudices and dense obtuseness of one who ought
to have seen more clearly his duty in this matter—that is
to say, of Meenie's father.

And so it was that, when the Monday morning came
round, Meenie had said good-bye to every one she knew,
and was ready to set out for the south. Not that she
was going by the mail. Oh no, Mr. Murray would not
hear of that, nor yet of her being sent in her father's
little trap. No; Mr. Murray placed his own large waggonette and a pair of horses at her disposal; and when
the mail-cart came along from Tongue, Mr. Blair's luggage
was quickly transferred to the more stately vehicle, and
immediately they started. She did not look like a girl
going away for a holiday. She was pale rather, and silent;
and Mr. Blair, who had memories of her as a bright,
merry, clear-eyed lass, could not understand why she
should be apparently so cast down at the thought of leaving her father's home for a mere month or so. As for old
John Murray, he went into the inn, grumbling and discontented.

'It is a strange thing,' he said,—for he was grieved and offended at their sending Meenie away, and he knew that Inver-Mudal would be a quite different place with her not there,—'a strange thing indeed to send a young girl away to Glasgow to get back the roses into her cheeks. Ay, will she get them there? A strange thing indeed. And her father a doctor too. It is just a teflle of a piece of nonsense.'

The worthy minister, on the other hand, was quite delighted to have so pretty a travelling companion with him on that long journey to the south; and he looked after her with the most anxious paternal solicitude, and from time to time he would try to cheer her with the recital of ancient Highland anecdotes that he had picked up during his fishing excursions. But he could see that the girl was preoccupied; her eyes were absent and her manner distraught; sometimes her colour came and went in a curious way, as if some sudden fancy had sent a tremor to her heart. Then, as they drew near to the great city—it was a pallid-clear morning, with some faint suggestions of blue overhead that gave the wan landscape an almost cheerful look—she was obviously suffering from nervous excitement; her answers to him were inconsequent, though she tried her bravest to keep up the conversation. The good man thought he would not bother her. No doubt it would be a great change—from the quiet of Inver-Mudal to the roar and bustle of the vast city; and no doubt the mere sight of hundreds and hundreds of strangers would in itself be bewildering. Meenie, as he understood, had been in Glasgow before, but it was some years ago, and she had not had a long experience of it; in any case, she would naturally be restless and nervous in looking forward to such a complete change in her way of life.

As they slowed into the station, moreover, he could not help observing how anxiously and eagerly she kept glancing from stranger to stranger, as they passed them on the platform.

'There will be somebody waiting for you, Miss Meenie?' he said at a venture.

'No, no,' she answered, somewhat hurriedly and shame-facedly as he thought—and the good minister was puzzled; 'Agatha wrote that Mr. Gemmill would be at the ware-house, and—and she would be busy in the house on a Monday morning, and I was just to take a cab and come on to Queen's Crescent. Oh! I shall manage all right,' she added, with some bravado.

And yet, when they had seen to their luggage, and got along to the platform outside the station, she seemed too bewildered to heed what was going on. Mr. Blair called a cab and got her boxes put on the top; but she was standing there by herself, looking up and down, and regarding the windows of the houses opposite in a kind of furtive and half-frightened way.

'This is Port Dundas Road?' she said to the minister (for had not Maggie, in her voluminous communications about Ronald, described the exact locality of his lodging, and the appearance of the station from his room?)

'It is.'

She hesitated for a second or two longer; and then, recalling herself with an effort, she thanked the minister for all his kindness, and bade him good-bye, and got into the cab. Of course she kept both windows down, so that she could command a view of both sides of the thorough-

fares as the man drove her away along the Cowcaddens
and the New City Road.   But alas ! how was she ever to
find Ronald—by accident, as she had hoped—in that continuous crowd?   She had pictured to herself her suddenly
meeting him face to face ; and she would read in his eyes
how much he remembered of Inver-Mudal and the olden
days.   But among this multitude, how was such a thing
possible ?   And then it was so necessary that this meeting
should be observed by no third person.

   However, these anxious doubts and fears were forcibly
driven from her head by her arrival at Queen's Crescent,
and the necessity of meeting the emergencies of the
moment.   She had but a half recollection of this secluded
little nook, with its semicircle of plain, neat, well-kept
houses, looking so entirely quiet and respectable ; and its
pretty little garden, with its grass-plots, and its flower-plots,
and its trim walks and fountain—all so nice and neat and
trim, and at this minute looking quite cheerful in the pallid
sunshine.   And here, awaiting her at the just opened door,
was her sister Agatha—a sonsy, sufficiently good-looking
young matron, who had inherited her buxom proportions
from her father, but had got her Highland eyes, which
were like Meenie's, from her mother.   And also there
were a smaller Agatha—a self-important little maiden of
ten—and two younger children ; and as the advent of this
pretty young aunt from Sutherlandshire was of great interest
to them, there was a babble of inquiries and answers as
they escorted her into the house.

   'And such a surprise to hear you were coming,' her
sister was saying.   'We little expected it—but ye're none
the less welcome—and Walter's just quite set up about it.
Ay, and ye're not looking so well, my father says ?—let's see.'

She took her by the shoulders and wheeled her to the light. But, of course, the girl was flushed with the excitement of her arrival, and pleased with the attentions of the little people, so that for the moment the expression of her face was bright enough.

'There's not much wrong,' said the sister, 'but I don't wonder at your being dull in yon dreadful hole. And I suppose there's no chance of moving now. If my father had only kept to Edinburgh or Glasgow, and got on like anybody else, we might all have been together, and among friends and acquaintances; but it was aye the same—give him the chance of a place where there was a gun or a fishing-rod handy, and that was enough. Well, well, Meenie, we must wake ye up a bit if you've been feeling dull; and Walter—he's as proud as a peacock that you're come; I declare it's enough to make any other woman than myself jealous, the way he shows your portrait to anybody and everybody that comes to the house; and I had a hint from him this morning that any bit things ye might need—mother's letter only came on Saturday—that they were to be a present from him, and there's nothing stingy about Wat, though I say it who shouldn't. And you'll have to share Aggie's bed for a night or two until we have· a room got ready for you.'

'If I had only known that I was going to put you about, Agatha——'

'Put us about, you daft lassie !' the elder sister exclaimed. 'Come away, and I'll show you where your things will have to' be stored for the present. And my father says there are to be no finishing lessons, or anything of that kind, for a while yet; you're to walk about and amuse yourself; and we've a family-ticket for the Botanic Gardens—you can

take a book there or some knitting; and then you'll have
to help me in the house, for Walter will be for showing you
off as his Highland sister-in-law, and we'll have plenty of
company.'

And so the good woman rattled on; and how abundantly
and secretly glad was Meenie that not a word was said of
Ronald Strang! She had felt guilty enough when she
entered the house; she had come on a secret errand that
she dared not disclose; and one or two things in her sister's
letters had convinced her that there were not likely to be
very friendly feelings towards Ronald in this little domestic
circle. But when they had gone over almost every conceivable topic, and not a single question had been asked
about Ronald, nor any reference even made to him, she
felt immensely relieved. To them, then, he was clearly of
no importance. Probably they had forgotten that she had
once or twice asked if he had called on them. Or perhaps
her sister had taken it for granted that the piece of news
she had sent concerning him would effectually and for ever
crush any interest in him that Meenie may have felt.
Anyhow, his name was not even mentioned; and that was
so far well.

But what a strange sensation was this—when in the
afternoon she went out for a stroll with the smaller Agatha
—to feel that at any moment, at the turning of any corner,
she might suddenly encounter Ronald. That ever-moving
crowd had the profoundest interest for her; these rather
grimy streets a continuous and mysterious fascination. Of
course the little Agatha, when they went forth from the
house, was for going up to the West End Park or out by
Hillhead to the Botanic Gardens, so that the pretty young
aunt should have a view of the beauties of Glasgow. But

Meenie had no difficulty in explaining that green slopes and trees and things of that kind had no novelty for her, whereas crowded streets and shops and the roar of cabs and carriages had; and so they turned city-wards when they left the house, and went away in by Cambridge Street and Sauchiehall Street to Buchanan Street. And was this the way, then, she asked herself (and she was rather an absent companion for her little niece), that Ronald would take on leaving his lodgings to get over to the south side of the city, where, as she understood from his sister's letters, lived the old forester who was superintending his studies? But there were so many people here!—and all seemingly strangers to each other; scarcely any two or three of them stopping to have a chat together; and all of them apparently in such a hurry. Argyll Street was even worse; indeed, she recoiled from that tumultuous thoroughfare; and the two of them turned north again. The lamplighter was beginning his rounds; here and there an orange star gleamed in the pallid atmosphere; here and there a shop window glowed yellow. When they got back to Queen's Crescent they found that Mr. Gemmill had returned; it was his tea-time; and there was a talk of the theatre for the older folk.

Well, she did not despair yet. For one thing, she had not been anxious to meet Ronald during that first plunge into the great city, for Agatha was with her. But that was merely because the little girl had obtained a holiday in honour of her aunt's coming; thereafter she went to school every morning; moreover, the household happened to be a maidservant short, and Mrs. Gemmill was busy, so that Meenie was left to do pretty much as she liked, and to go about alone. And her walks did not take her much to the Botanic Gardens, nor yet to the West End Park and Kelvin

Grove; far rather she preferred to go errands for her sister, and often these would take her in by Sauchiehall Street and the top of Buchanan Street; and always her eyes were anxious and yet timorous, seeking and yet half-fearing to find. But where was Ronald? She tried different hours. She grew to know every possible approach to that lodging in the Port Dundas Road. And she had schooled herself now so that she could search long thoroughfares with a glance that was apparently careless enough; and she had so often pictured to herself their meeting, that she knew she would not exhibit too great a surprise nor make too open a confession of her joy.

And at last her patient waiting was rewarded. It was in Renfield Street that she suddenly caught sight of him—a long way off he was, but coming towards her, and all unconscious of her being there. For a moment her schooling of herself gave way somewhat; for her heart was beating so wildly as almost to choke her; and she went on with her eyes fixed on the ground, wondering what she should say, wondering if he would find her face grown paler than it used to be, wondering what he would think of her having sent him the bit of white heather. And then she forced herself to raise her eyes; and it was at the very same instant that he caught sight of her—though he was yet some distance off—and for the briefest moment she saw his strange and startled look. But what was this? Perhaps he fancied she had not seen him; perhaps he had reasons for not wishing to be seen; at all events, after that one swift recognition of her, he had suddenly slunk away—down some lane or other—and when she went forward, in rather a blind and bewildered fashion, behold! there was no Ronald there at all. She looked around—with a heart as if turned to stone—but there was no trace of him. And then she went on, rather proudly—or perhaps, rather, trying to feel proud and hurt; but there was a gathering mist coming into her eyes; and she scarcely knew—nor cared— whither she was walking.

CHAPTER IV.

A BOLDER STEP.

As for him, he slunk aside hurriedly and all abashed and dismayed. He did not pause until he was safe away from any pursuit; and there was a lowering expression on his face, and his hand shook a little. He could only hope that she had not seen him. Instantly he had seen her, he knew that he dared not meet the beautiful clear eyes, that would regard him, and perhaps mutely ask questions of him, even if there was no indignant reproach in them. For during these past few days he had gradually been becoming conscious of the squalor and degradation into which he had sunk; and sometimes he would strive to raise himself out of that; and sometimes he would sink back despairing, careless of what might become of him or his poor affairs. But always there was there in his room that mystic white token that Meenie had sent him; and at least it kept him thinking—his conscience was not allowed to slumber; and sometimes it became so strong an appeal to him—that is to say, he read into the message such wild and daring and fantastic possibilities—that he would once more resume that terrible struggle with the iron bands of habit that bound him.

'What is the matter wi' Ronald?' Kate Menzies asked

of her cronies. ' He hasna been near the house these three
or four days.'

' I'm thinking he's trying to earn the Blue Ribbon,' said
old Mr. Jaap.

' And no thriving weel on't, poor lad,' said Jimmy Laidlaw. ' Down in the mouth 's no the word. He's just like
the ghost o' himsel'.'

' I tell ye what, Mistress,' said the big skipper, who was
contemplating with much satisfaction a large beaker of hot
rum and water, ' the best thing you could do would be just
to take the lad in hand, and marry him right off. He
would have somebody to look after him, and so would you;
as handsome a couple as ever stepped along Jamaica Street,
I'll take my oath.'

The buxom widow laughed and blushed; but she was
bound to protest.

' Na, na, Captain, I ken better than that. I'm no
going to throw away a business like this on any man. I'll
bide my ain mistress for a while longer, if ye please.'

And then mother Paterson—who had a handy gift of
facile acquiescence—struck in—

' That's right, Katie dear! Ye're sich a wise woman.
To think ye'd throw away a splendid place like this, and a
splendid business, on any man, and make him maister! And
how long would it be before he ate and drank ye out o' house
and ha'?—set him up with a handsome wife and a splendid business thrown at his heed, and scarcely for the asking!
Na, na, Katie, woman, ye ken your own affairs better than
that ; ye're no for any one to come in and be maister here.'

' But I'm concerned about the lad,' said Kate Menzies,
a little absently. ' He met wi' none but friends here. He
might fa' into worse hands.'

'Gang up yersel', Mistress, and hae a talk wi' him,' said the skipper boldly.

Kate Menzies did not do that; but the same evening she wrote Ronald a brief note. And very well she could write too—in a dashing, free handwriting; and gilt-edged was the paper, and rose-pink was the envelope.

'DEAR RONALD—Surely there is no quarrel between us. If I have offended you, come and tell me; don't go away and sulk. If I have done or said anything to offend you, I will ask your pardon. Can I do anything more than that? Your cousin and friend,

'KATE MENZIES.'

Of course he had to answer such an appeal in person: he went down the next morning.

'Quarrel, woman? What put that into your head? If there had been anything of that kind, I would have told you fast enough; I'm not one of the sulking kind.'

'Well, I'm very glad to ken we're just as good friends as before,' said Kate, regarding him, 'but I'm not glad to see the way ye're looking, Ronald, my lad. Ye're not yourself at all, my man—what's got ye whitey-faced, limp, shaky-looking like that? See here.'

She went to the sideboard, and the next instant there was on the table a bottle of champagne, with a couple of glasses, and a flask of angostura bitters.

'No, no, Katie, lass, I will not touch a drop,' said he: and he rose and took his cap in his hand.

'You will not?' she said. 'You will not? Why, man, you're ill—you're ill, I tell ye. It's medicine!'

He gripped her by the hand, and took the bottle from her, and put it down on the table.

'If I'm ill, I deserve to be, and that's the fact, lass. Let be—let be, woman; I'm obliged to ye—some other time—some other time.'

'Then if you winna, I will,' she said, and she got hold of the bottle and opened it and poured out a glass of the foaming fluid.

'And dinna I ken better what's good for ye than ye do yersel'?' said she boldly. 'Ay, if ye were ruled by me, and drank nothing but what ye get in this house, there would be little need for ye to be frightened at what a wean might drink. Ye dinna ken your best friends, my lad.'

'I know you wish me weel, Katie, lass,' said he, for he did not wish to appear ungrateful, 'but I'm better without it.'

'Yes,' said she tauntingly. 'Ye're better without sitting up a' night wi' a lot o' roystering fellows, smoking bad tobacco and drinking bad whisky. What mak's your face sae white? It's fusel-oil, if ye maun ken. Here, Ronald, what canna hurt a woman canna hurt a man o' your build—try it, and see if ye dinna feel better.'

She put a good dash of bitters into the glass, and poured out the champagne, and offered it to him. He did not wish to offend her; and he himself did not believe the thing could hurt him; he took the glass and sipped about a teaspoonful, and then set it down.

Kate Menzies looked at him, and laughed aloud, and took him by the shoulders and pushed him back into his chair.

'There's a man for ye! Whatna young ladies' seminary have ye been brought up at?'

'I'll tell ye, lass,' he retorted. 'It was one where they taught folk no to force other folk to drink against their will.'

'Then it was different frae the one where I was brought up, for there, when the doctor ordered anybody to take medicine, they were made to take it. And here's yours,' she said; and she stood before him with the glass in her hand. She was good-natured; it would have been ungracious to refuse; he took the glass from her and drank off the contents.

Now a glass of champagne, even with the addition of a little angostura bitters, cannot be called a very powerful potion to those accustomed to such things; but the fact was that he had not touched a drop of any alcoholic fluid for two days; and this seemed to go straight to the brain. It produced a slight, rather agreeable giddiness; a sense of comfort was diffused throughout the system; he was not so anxious to get away. And Kate began talking—upbraiding him for thinking that she wanted to see him otherwise than well and in his usual health, and declaring that if he were guided by her, there would be no need for him to torture himself with total abstinence, and to reduce himself to this abject state. The counsel (which was meant in all honesty) fell on yielding ears; Kate brought some biscuits, and filled herself out another glass.

'That's what it is,' she said boldly, 'if you would be ruled by my advice there would be no shaking hands and white cheeks for ye. Feeling better, are ye?—ay, I warrant ye! Here, man, try this.'

She filled his glass again, adding a good dose of bitters.

'This one I will, but not a drop more,' said he. 'Ye're a desperate creature, lass, for making folk comfortable.'

'I ken what's the matter wi' you better than ye ken yoursel', Ronald,' said she, looking at him shrewdly. 'You're disappointed — you're out o' heart — because thae fine

American friends o' yours hae forgotten you ; and you've got sick o' this new work o' yours ; and you've got among a lot o' wild fellows that are leading ye to the devil. Mark my words. Americans ! Better let a man trust to his ain kith and kin.'

' Well, Katie, lass, I maun say this, that ye've just been ower kind to me since ever I came to Glasgow.'

' Another glass, Ronald——'

' Not one drop—thank ye '—and this time he rose with the definite resolve to get away, for even these two glasses had caused a swimming in his head, and he knew not how much more he might drink if he stayed.

' Better go for a long walk, then,' said Kate, ' and come back at three and have dinner with us. I'll soon put ye on your legs again—trust to me.'

But when he went out into the open air, he found himself so giddy and half-dazed and bewildered that, instead of going away for any long walk, he thought he would go back home and lie down. He felt less happy now. Why had he taken this accursed thing after all his resolves ?

And then it was—as he went up Renfield Street—that he caught his first glimpse of Meenie. No wonder he turned and slunk rapidly away—anxious to hide anywhere —hoping that Meenie had not seen him. And what a strange thing was this—Meenie in Glasgow town ! Oh, if he could only be for a single day as once he had been—as she had known him in the happy times when life went by like a laugh and a song—how wonderful it would be to go along these thoroughfares hoping every moment to catch sight of her face ! A dull town ?—no, a radiant town, with music in the air, and joy and hope shining down from the skies ! But now—he was a cowering fugitive—sick in body and sick in mind—trembling with the excitement of this sudden meeting—and anxious above all other things that he should get back to the seclusion of his lodging unseen.

Well, he managed that, at all events; and there he sate down, wondering over this thing that had just happened. Meenie in Glasgow town!—and why? And why had she sent him the white heather? Nay, he could not doubt but that she had heard; and that this was at once a message of reproach and an appeal; and what answer had he to give supposing that some day or other he should meet her face to face? How could he win back to his former state, so that he should not be ashamed to meet those clear, kind eyes? If there were but some penance now—no matter what suffering it entailed—that would obliterate these last months and restore him to himself, how gladly would he welcome that! But it was not only the bodily sickness— he believed he could mend that; he had still a fine physique; and surely absolute abstention from stimulants, no matter with what accompanying depression, would in time give him back his health—it was mental sickness and hopelessness and remorse that had to be cured; and how was that to be attempted? Or why should he attempt it? What care had he for the future? To be sure, he would stop drinking, definitely; and he would withdraw himself from those wild companions; and he would have a greater regard for his appearance; so that, if he should by chance meet Meenie face to face, he would not have to be altogether so ashamed. But after? When she had gone away again? For of course he assumed that she was merely here on a visit.

And all this time he was becoming more and more con-

scious of how far he had fallen—of the change that had
come over himself and his circumstances in these few
months; and a curious fancy got into his head that he
would like to try to realise what he had been like in those
former days.   He got out his blotting-pad of fragments—
not those dedicated to Meenie, that had been carefully put
aside—and about the very first of them that he chanced to
light upon, when he looked down the rough lines, made
him exclaim—

'God bless me, was I like *that*—and no longer ago than
last January?'

The piece was called 'A Winter Song'; and surely the
man who could write in this gay fashion had an abundant
life and joy and hope in his veins, and courage to face the
worst bleakness of the winter, and a glad looking-forward to
the coming of the spring?

> *Keen blows the wind upon Clebrig's side,*
> *And the snow lies thick on the heather:*
> *And the shivering hinds are glad to hide*
> *Away from the winter weather.*
>
> Chorus: *But soon the birds will begin to sing,*
> *And we will sing too, my dear,*
> *To give good welcoming to the spring,*
> *In the primrose time o' the year!*
>
> *Hark how the black lake, torn and tost,*
> *Thunders along its shores;*
> *And the burn is hard in the grip of the frost,*
> *And white, snow-white are the moors.*
>
> Chorus: *But soon the birds will begin to sing, etc.*
>
> *O then the warm west winds will blow,*
> *And all in the sunny weather,*
> *It's over the moorlands we will go,*
> *You and I, my love, together.*

Chorus : *And then the birds will begin to sing,*
And we will sing too, my dear,
To give good welcoming to the spring,
In the primrose-time o' the year!

Why, surely the blood must have been dancing in his brain when he wrote that; and the days white and clear around him; and life merry and hopeful enough. And now? Well, it was no gladdening thing to think of: he listlessly put away the book.

And then he rose and went and got a pail of water and thrust his head into that—for he was glad to feel that this muzzy sensation was going; and thereafter he dried and brushed his hair with a little more care than usual; and put on a clean collar. Nay, he began to set the little room to rights—and his life in Highland lodges had taught him how to do that about as well as any woman could; and he tried to brighten the window panes a little, to make the place look more cheerful; and he arranged the things on the mantel-shelf in better order— with the bit of white heather in the middle. Then he came to his briar-root pipe; and paused. He took it up, hesitating.

'Yes, my friend, you must go too,' he said, with firm lips; and he deliberately broke it, and tossed the fragments into the grate.

And then he remembered that it was nearly three o'clock, and as he feared that Kate Menzies might send some one of her friends to fetch him, or even come for him herself, he put on his cap, and took a stick in his hand, and went out. In half an hour or so he had left the city behind him and was lost in that melancholy half-country that lies around it on the north; but he cared little now how the landscape looked; he was wondering what had brought Meenie to Glasgow town, and whether she had seen him, and what she had heard of him. And at Inver-Mudal too? Well, they might think the worst of him there if they chose. But had Meenie heard?

He scarcely knew how far he went; but in the dusk of the evening he was again approaching the city by the Great Western Road; and as he came nearer to the houses, he found that the lamps were lit, and the great town settling down into the gloom of the night. Now he feared no detection; and so it was that when he arrived at Melrose Street he paused there. Should he venture into Queen's Crescent?—it was but a stone's throw away. For he guessed that Meenie must be staying with her sister; and he knew the address that she had given him, though he had never called; nay, he had had the curiosity, once or twice in passing, to glance at the house; and easily enough he could now make it out if he chose. He hesitated for a second or two; then he stealthily made his way along the little thoroughfare; and entered the crescent—but keeping to the opposite side from Mrs. Gemmill's dwelling—and there quietly walked up and down. He could see the windows well enough; they were all of them lit; and the house seemed warm and comfortable; Meenie would be at home there, and among friends, and her bright laugh would be heard from room to room. Perhaps they had company too—since all the windows were ablaze; rich folk, no doubt, for the Gemmills were themselves well-to-do people; and Meenie would be made much of by these strangers, and they would come round her, and the beautiful Highland eyes would be turned towards them, and they would hear her speak in her quiet, gentle, quaint way. Nor was there any trace of envy or jealousy in this man's composition—

outcast as he now deemed himself. Jealousy of Meenie?
—why, he wished the bountiful heavens to pour their
choicest blessings upon her, and the winds to be for ever
soft around her, and all sweet and gracious things to await
her throughout her girlhood and her womanhood and her
old age. No; it did not trouble him that these rich folk
were fortunate enough to be with her, to listen to her, to
look at the clear, frank eyes; it might have troubled him
had he thought that they might not fully understand the
generous rose-sweetness of her nature, nor fully appreciate
her straightforward, unconscious simplicity, nor be sufficiently kind to her. And it was scarcely necessary to consider that; of course they all of them would be kind to
her, for how could they help it?

But his guess that they might be entertaining friends
was wrong. By and by a cab drove up; in a few minutes
the door was opened; he ventured to draw a little nearer;
and then he saw three figures—one of them almost
assuredly Meenie—come out and enter the vehicle. They
drove off; no doubt they were going to some concert or
theatre, he thought; and he was glad that Meenie was being
amused and entertained so; and was among friends. And
as for himself?—

'Well,' he was inwardly saying, as he resumed his walk
homeward, 'the dreams that look so fine when one is up
among the hills are knocked on the head sure enough when
one comes to a town. I'll have no more to do with these
books; nor with the widow Menzies and her friends either.
To-morrow morning I'm off to the recruiting-sergeant—
that's the best thing for me now.'

By the time he had got home he was quite resolved upon
this. But there was a note lying there on the table for him.

'That woman again,' he said to himself. 'Katie, lass, I'm afraid you and I must part, but I hope we'll part good friends.'

And then his eyes grew suddenly startled. He took up the note, staring at the outside, apparently half afraid. And then he opened it and read—but in a kind of wild and breathless bewilderment—these two or three lines, written in rather a shaky hand—

'DEAR RONALD—I wish to see you. Would it trouble you to be at the corner of Sauchiehall Street and Renfield Street to-morrow morning at eleven?—I will not detain you more than a few minutes. Yours sincerely,

'MEENIE DOUGLAS.'

There was not much sleep for him that night.

CHAPTER V.

A MEETING.

INDEED there was no sleep at all for him that night. He knew not what this summons might mean; and all the assurance and self-confidence of former days was gone now; he was nervous, distracted, easily alarmed; ready to imagine evil things; and conscious that he was in no fit state to present himself before Meenie. And yet he never thought of slinking away. Meenie desired to see him, and that was enough. Always and ever he had been submissive to her slightest wish. And if it were merely to reproach him, to taunt him with his weakness and folly, that she had now sent for him, he would go all the same. He deserved that and more. If only it had been some one else—not Meenie—whose resolute clear eyes he had to meet!

That brief interview over—and then for the Queen's shilling: this was what was before him now, and the way seemed clear enough. But so unnerved was he that the mere idea of having to face this timid girl made him more and more restless and anxious; and at last, towards three o'clock in the morning, he, not having been to bed at all, opened the door and stole down the stair and went out into the night. The black heavens were pulsating from time to time with a lurid red sent over from the ironworks

in the south; somewhere there was the footfall of a
policeman unseen; the rest was darkness and a terrible
silence. He wandered away through the lonely streets, he
scarcely knew whither. He was longing that the morning
should come, and yet dreading its approach. He reached
the little thoroughfare that leads into Queen's Crescent;
but he held on his way without turning aside; it was not
for this poor trembling ghost and coward to pass under
her window, with 'Sleep dwell upon thine eyes, peace in
thy breast' as his unspoken benediction. .He held on his
way towards the open country, wandering quite aimlessly,
and busy only with guesses and forebodings and hopeless
desires that he might suddenly find before him the dark-
rolling waters of Lethe, and plunge into them, and wash
away from him all knowledge and recollection of the past.
When at length he turned towards the city, the .gray dawn
was breaking in the dismal skies; the first of the milk-carts
came slowly crawling into the town; and large waggons
laden with vegetables and the like. He got back to his
lodgings; threw himself on the bed; and there had an
hour or two of broken and restless sleep.

When he awoke he went quickly to the window. The
skies were heavy; there was a dull drizzle in the thick
atmosphere; the pavements were wet. It was with a
sudden sense of relief that he saw what kind of a day it was.
Of course Meenie would never think of coming out on so
wet and miserable a morning. He would keep the appointment, doubtless; she would not appear—taking it for
granted he would not expect her; and then—then for the
recruiting-sergeant and a final settlement of all these ills
and shames. Nevertheless he dressed himself with scrupu-
lous neatness; and brushed and rebrushed his clothes;

and put on his deerstalker's cap—for the sake of old days.
And then, just as he was leaving, he took a little bit of
the white heather, and placed it in his waistcoat pocket;
if the talisman had any subtle power whatever, all the good
luck that he could wish for was to find Meenie not too
bitter in her scorn.

He made his way to the corner of Sauchiehall Street
some little time before the appointed hour. But it was
actually raining now; of course Meenie would not come.
So he idly paced up and down; staring absently at the
shop windows; occasionally looking along the street, but
with no great expectation; and thinking how well content
and satisfied with themselves these people seemed to be
who were now hurrying by under their streaming umbrellas.
His thoughts went far afield. Vimiera—Salamanca—Ciudad
Rodrigo — Balaklava — Alma — Lucknow — Alumbagh —
these were the names and memories that were in his head.
An old school companion of his own had got the V.C. for
a conspicuous act of daring at the storming of the Redan,
and if that were not likely to be his proud fate, at least
in this step he was resolved upon he would find safety and
a severance from degrading bonds, and a final renunciation
of futile ambitions and foolish and idle dreams.

He was looking into a bookseller's window. A timid
hand touched his arm.

'Ronald!'

And oh! the sudden wonder and the thrill of finding
before him those beautiful, friendly, glad eyes, so true, so
frank, so full of all womanly tenderness and solicitude,
and abundant and obvious kindness! Where was the
reproach of them? They were full of a kind of half-
hidden joy—timid and reluctant, perhaps, a little—but

honest and clear and unmistakable; and as for him—well, his breath was clean taken away by the surprise, and by the sudden revulsion of feeling from a listless despair to the consciousness that Meenie was still his friend; and all he could do was to take the gentle hand in both of his and hold it fast.

'I—I heard that you were not—not very well, Ronald,' she managed to say.

And then the sound of her voice—that brought with it associations of years—seemed to break the spell that was on him.

'Bless me, Miss Douglas,' he said, 'you will get quite wet! Will you not put up your umbrella—or—or take shelter somewhere?'

'Oh, I do not mind the rain,' she said, and there was a kind of tremulous laugh about her lips, as if she were trying to appear very happy indeed. 'I do not mind the rain. We did not heed the rain much at Inver-Mudal, Ronald, when there was anything to be done. And—and so glad I am to see you! It seems so long a time since you left the Highlands.'

'Ay; and it has been a bad time for me,' he said; and now he was beginning to get his wits together again. He could not keep Miss Douglas thus standing in the wet. He would ask her why she had sent for him; and then he would bid her good-bye and be off; but with a glad, glad heart that he had seen her even for these few seconds.

'And there are so many things to be talked over after so long a time,' said she; 'I hope you have a little while to spare, Ronald——'

'But to keep you in the rain, Miss Douglas——'

'Oh, but this will do,' said she (and whatever her inward

thoughts were, her speech was blithe enough). 'See, I
will put up the umbrella, and you will carry it for me—it is
not the first time, Ronald, that you and I have had to walk
in the rain together, and without any umbrella. And do
you know why I do not care for the rain?' she added,
glancing at him again with the frank, affectionate eyes;
'it's because I am so glad to find you looking not so ill
after all, Ronald.'

'Not so ill, maybe, as I deserve to be,' he answered;
but he took the umbrella and held it over her; and they
went down Renfield Street a little way and then into West
Regent Street; and if she did not put her hand on his arm,
at least she was very close to him, and the thrill of the touch
of her dress was magnetic and strange. Strange, indeed;
and strange that he should find himself walking side by side
with Meenie through the streets of Glasgow town; and
listening mutely and humbly the while to all her varied talk
of what had happened since he left Inver-Mudal. Whatever she had heard of him, it seemed to be her wish to
ignore that. She appeared to assume that their relations to
each other now were just as they had been in former days.
And she was quite bright and cheerful and hopeful; how
could he know that the first glance at his haggard face had
struck like a dagger to her heart?

Moreover, the rain gradually ceased; the umbrella was
lowered; a light west wind was quietly stirring; and by
and by a warmer light began to interfuse itself through the
vaporous atmosphere. Nay, by the time they had reached
Blythswood Square, a pallid sunshine was clearly shining
on the wet pavements and door-steps and house-fronts; and
far overhead, and dimly seen through the mysteriously
moving pall of mist and smoke, there were faint touches of

blue, foretelling the opening out to a joyfuller day. The wide square was almost deserted; they could talk to each other as they chose; though, indeed, the talking was mostly on her side. Something, he scarcely knew what, kept him silent and submissive; but his heart was full of gratitude towards her; and from time to time—for how could he help it?—some chance word or phrase of appeal would bring him face to face with Meenie's eyes.

So far she had cunningly managed to avoid all reference to his own affairs, so that he might get accustomed to this friendly conversation; but at length she said—

'And now about yourself, Ronald?'

'The less said the better,' he answered. 'I wish that I had never come to this town.'

'What?' she said, with a touch of remonstrance in her look. 'Have you so soon forgotten the fine prospects you started away with? Surely not! Why, it was only the other day I had a letter from Miss Hodson—the young American lady, you remember—and she was asking all about you, and whether you had passed the examination yet; and she said her father and herself were likely to come over next spring, and hoped to hear you had got the certificate.'

He seemed to pay no heed to this news.

'I wish I had never left Inver-Mudal,' he said. 'I was content there; and what more can a man wish for anywhere? It's little enough of that I've had since I came to this town. But for whatever has happened to me, I've got myself to blame; and—and I beg your pardon, Miss Douglas, I will not bother you with any poor concerns of mine——'

'But if I wish to be bothered?' she said quickly. 'Ronald, do you know why I have come from the Highlands?'

Her face was blushing a rosy red; but her eyes were steadfast and clear and kind; and she had stopped in her walk to confront him.

'I heard the news of you—yes, I heard the news,' she continued; and it was his eyes, not hers, that were down-cast; 'and I knew you would do much for me—at least, I thought so,—and I said to myself that if I were to go to Glasgow, and find you, and ask you for my sake to give me a promise——'

'I know what ye would say, Miss Douglas,' he inter-posed, for she was dreadfully embarrassed. 'To give up the drink. Well, it's easily promised and easily done, *now* —indeed, I've scarce touched a drop since ever I got the bit of heather you sent me. It was a kind thing to think of —maybe I'm making too bold to think it was you that sent it——'

'I knew you would know that it was I that sent it—I meant you to know,' she said simply.

'It was never any great love of the drink that drove me that way,' he said. 'I think it was that I might be able to forget for a while.'

'To forget what, Ronald?' she asked, regarding him.

'That ever I was such a fool as to leave the only people I cared for,' he answered frankly, 'and come away here among strangers, and bind myself to strive for what I had no interest in. But bless me, Miss Douglas, to think I should keep ye standing here—talking about my poor affairs——'

'Ronald,' she said calmly, 'do you know that I have come all the way to Glasgow to see you and to talk about your affairs and nothing else; and you are not going to hurry away? Tell me about yourself. What are you doing? Are you getting on with your studies?'.

He shook his head.

'No, no.   I have lost heart that way altogether.   Many's the time I have thought of writing to Lord Ailine, and asking to be taken back, if it was only to look after the dogs. I should never have come to this town; and now I am going away from it, for good.'

'Going away?   Where?' she said, rather breathlessly.

'I want to make a clean break off from the kind of life I have been leading,' said he, 'and I know the surest way. I mean to enlist into one of the Highland regiments that's most likely to be ordered off on foreign service.'

'Ronald!'

She seized his hand and held it.

'Ronald, you will not do that!'

Well, he was startled by the sudden pallor of her face; and bewildered by the entreaty so plainly visible in the beautiful eyes; and perhaps he did not quite know how he answered.   But he spoke quickly.

'Oh, of course I will not do that,' he said, 'of course I will not do that, Miss Douglas, so long as you are in Glasgow.   How could I?   Why, the chance of seeing you, even at a distance—for a moment even—I would wait days for that.   When I made up my mind to enlist, I had no thought that I might ever have the chance of seeing you. Oh no; I will wait until you have gone back to the High-lands—how could I go away from Glasgow and miss any single chance of seeing you, if only for a moment?'

'Yes, yes,' she said eagerly, 'you will do nothing until then, anyway; and in the meantime I shall see you often——'

His face lighted up with surprise.

'Will you be so kind as that?' he said quickly.   And

then he dropped her hand. 'No, no. I am so bewildered
by the gladness of seeing you that—that I forgot. Let me
go my own way. You were always so generous in your
good nature that you spoiled us all at Inver-Mudal ; here
—here it is different. You are living with your sister, I
suppose? and of course you have many friends, and many
things to do and places to visit. You must not trouble
about me ; but as long as you are in Glasgow—well, there
will always be the chance of my catching a glimpse of you
—and if you knew what it was—to me——'

But here he paused abruptly, fearful of offending by
confessing too much ; and now they had resumed their
leisurely walking along the half-dried pavements ; and
Meenie was revolving certain little schemes and artifices in
her brain—with a view to their future meeting. And the
morning had grown so much brighter ; and there was a
pleasant warmth of sunlight in the air ; and she was glad
to know that at least for a time Ronald would not be
leaving the country. She turned to him with a smile.

'I shall have to be going back home now,' she said,
'but you will not forget, Ronald, that you have made me
two promises this morning.'

'It's little you know, Miss Douglas,' said he, 'what I
would do for you, if I but knew what ye wished. I mean
for you yourself. For my own self, I care but little what
happens to me. I have made a mistake in my life somehow. I——'

'Then will you promise me more, Ronald?' said she
quickly ; for she would not have him talk in that strain.

'What?'

'Will you make me a promise that you will not enlist at
all?'

'I will, if it is worth heeding one way or the other.'

'But make me the promise,' said she, and she regarded him with no unfriendly eyes.

'There's my hand on't.'

'And another—that you will work hard and try and get the forestry certificate?'

'What's the use of that, lass?' said he, forgetting his respect for her. 'I have put all that away now. That's all away beyond me now.'

'No,' she said proudly. 'No. It is not. Oh, do you think that the people who know you do not know what your ability is? Do you think they have lost their faith in you? Do you think they are not still looking forward and hoping the time may come that they may be proud of your success, and—and—come and shake hands with you, Ronald—and say how glad they are? And have you no regard for them, or heed for their—their affection towards you?'

Her cheeks were burning red, but she was far too much in earnest to measure her phrases; and she held his hand in an imploring kind of way; and surely, if ever a brave and unselfish devotion and love looked out from a woman's eyes, that was the message that Meenie's eyes had for him then.

'I had a kind of fancy,' he said, 'that if I could get abroad—with one o' those Highland regiments—there might come a time when I could have the chance of winning the V.C.—the Victoria Cross, I mean; ay, and it would have been a proud day for me the day that I was able to send that home to you.'

'To me, Ronald?' she said, rather faintly.

'Yes, yes,' said he. 'Whatever happened to me after that day would not matter much.'

'But you have promised——'

'And I will keep that promise, and any others you may ask of me, Miss Douglas.'

''That you will call me Meenie, for one?' she said, quite simply and frankly.

'No, no; I could not do that,' he answered—and yet the permission sounded pleasant to the ear.

'We are old friends, Ronald,' she said. 'But that is a small matter. Well, now, I must be getting back home; and yet I should like to see you again soon, Ronald, for there are so many things I have to talk over with you. Will you come and see my sister?'

His hesitation and embarrassment were so obvious that she instantly repented her of having thrown out this invitation; moreover, it occurred to herself that there would be little chance of her having any private speech of Ronald (which was of such paramount importance at this moment) if he called at Queen's Crescent.

'No, not yet,' she said, rather shamefacedly and with downcast eyes; 'perhaps, since—since there are one or two private matters to talk over, we—we could meet just as now? It is not—taking up too much of your time, Ronald?'

'Why,' said he, 'if I could see you for a moment, any day—merely to say "good morning"—that would be a well-spent day for me; no more than that used to make many a long day quite happy for me at Inver-Mudal.'

'Could you be here to-morrow at eleven, Ronald?' she asked, looking up shyly.

'Yes, yes, and gladly!' he answered; and presently they had said good-bye to each other; and she had set out for Queen's Crescent by herself; while he turned towards the east.

And now all his being seemed transfused with joy and
deep gratitude; and the day around him was clear and
sweet and full of light; and all the world seemed swinging
onward in an ether of happiness and hope. The dreaded
interview!—where was the reproach and scorn of it?
Instead of that it had been all radiant with trust and
courage and true affection; and never had Meenie's eyes
been so beautiful and solicitous with all good wishes; never
had her voice been so strangely tender, every tone of it
seeming to reach the very core of his heart. And how was
he to requite her for this bountiful care and sympathy—
that overawed him almost when he came to think of it?
Nay, repayment of any kind was all impossible: where was
the equivalent of such generous regard? But at least he
could faithfully observe the promises he had made—yes,
these and a hundred more; and perhaps this broken life of
his might still be of some small service, if in any way it
could win for him a word of Meenie's approval.

And then, the better to get away from temptation, and
to cut himself wholly adrift from his late companions, he
walked home to his lodgings and packed up his few things
and paid his landlady a fortnight's rent in lieu of notice,
as had been agreed upon. That same night he was established in new quarters, in the Garscube Road; and he had
left no address behind him; so that if Kate Menzies, or
the skipper, or any of his cronies of the Harmony Club
were to wonder at his absence and seek to hunt him out,
they would seek and hunt in vain.

CHAPTER VI.

THAT night he slept long and soundly, and his dreams were all about Inver-Mudal and the quiet life among the hills; and, strangely enough, he fancied himself there, and Meenie absent; and always he was wondering when she was coming back from Glasgow town, and always he kept looking for her as each successive mail-cart came through from the south. And then in the morning, when he awoke, and found himself in the great city itself, and knew that Meenie was there too, and that in a few hours they were to meet, his heart was filled with joy, and the day seemed rich and full of promise, and the pale and sickly sunlight that struggled in through the window panes and lit up the dusty little room seemed a glorious thing, bringing with it all glad tidings. 'You, fortunate Glasgow town!' he had rhymed in the olden days; and this was the welcome that Glasgow town had for Meenie—sunlight, and perhaps a glimpse of blue here and there, and a light west wind blowing in from the heights of Dowanhill and Hillhead.

He dressed with particular care; and if his garments were not of the newest fashionable cut, at least they clung with sufficient grace and simplicity of outline to the manly and well-set figure. And he knew himself that he was looking less

haggard than on the previous day. He was feeling altogether
better; the long and sound sleep had proved a powerful
restorative; and his heart was light with hope. The happy
sunlight shining out there on the gray pavements and the
gray fronts of the houses!—was there ever in all the world
a fairer and joyfuller city than this same Glasgow town?

He was in Blythswood Square long before the appointed
hour; and she also was a little early. But this time it was
Meenie who was shy and embarrassed; she was not so
earnest and anxious as she had been the day before, for
much of her errand was now satisfactorily accomplished;
and when, after a moment's hesitation, he asked her whether
she would not go and have a look at the terraces and trees
in the West End Park, it seemed so like two lovers setting
out for a walk together that the conscious blood mantled in
her checks, and her eyes were averted. But she strove to
be very business-like; and asked him a number of questions
about Mr. Weems; and wondered that the Americans had
said nothing further about the purchase of an estate in the
Highlands, of which there had been some little talk. In
this way—and with chance remarks and inquiries about
Maggie, and the Reverend Andrew, and Mr. Murray, and
Harry the terrier, and what not—they made their way
through various thoroughfares until they reached the tall
gates of the West End Park.

Here there was much more quietude than in those noisy
streets; and when they had walked along one of the wide
terraces, until they came to a seat partly surrounded by
shrubs, Meenie suggested that they might sit down there,
for she wished to reason seriously with him. He smiled a
little; but he was very plastic in her hands. Nay, was it
not enough merely to hear Meenie speak—no matter what

the subject might be? And then he was sitting by her side, with all that wide prospect stretched out before them—the spacious terraces, the groups of trees, the curving river, and the undulating hills beyond.   It was a weird kind of a morning, moreover; for the confused and wan sunlight kept struggling through the ever-changing mist, sometimes throwing a coppery radiance on the late autumn foliage, or again shining pale and silver-like as the fantastic cloud-wreaths slowly floated onward.   The view before them was mysterious and vast because of its very vagueness; and even the new University buildings—over there on the heights above the river—looked quite imposing and picturesque, for they loomed large and dusky and remote through the bewildering sunlit haze.

'Now, Ronald,' she said, 'I want you to tell me how it was you came to lose heart so, and to give up what you undertook to do when you left Inver-Mudal. Why, when you left you were full of such high hopes; and every one was sure of your success; and you were all anxiety to begin.'

'That's true, Miss Douglas,' he answered, rather absently. 'I think my head must have been in a kind of a whirl at that time.   It seemed so fine and easy a thing to strive for ; and I did not stop to ask what use it would be to me, sup-posing I got it.'

'The use?' she said.   'A better position for yourself— isn't it natural to strive for that?   And perhaps, if you did not care much to have more money for yourself—for you have very strange notions, Ronald, about some things— you must see how much kindness can be done to others by people who are well off.   I don't understand you at all——'

'Well, then,' said he, shifting his ground, 'I grew sick

and tired of the town life. I was never meant for that. Every day——'

'But, Ronald,' she said, interrupting him in a very definite tone of remonstrance, 'you knew that your town life was only a matter of months! And the harder you worked the sooner it would be over! What reason was that?'

'There may have been other reasons,' he said, but rather unwillingly.

'What were they?'

. 'I cannot tell you.'

'Ronald,' she said, and the touch of wounded pride in her voice thrilled him strangely, 'I have come all the way from the Highlands—and—and done what few girls would have done—for your sake; and yet you will not be frank with me—when all that I want is to see you going straight towards a happier future.'

'I dare not tell you, you would be angry.'

'I am not given to anger,' she answered, calmly, and yet with a little surprised resentment. For she could but imagine that this was some entanglement of debt, or something of the kind, of which he was ashamed to speak; and yet, unless she knew clearly the reasons that had induced him to abandon the project that he had undertaken so eagerly, how was she to argue with him and urge him to resume it?

'Well, then, we'll put it this way,' said he, after a second or two of hesitation—and his face was a little pale, and his eyes were fixed on her with an anxious nervousness, so that, at the first sign of displeasure, he could instantly stop. 'There was a young lass that I knew there—in the Highlands—and she was, oh yes, she was out of my station

altogether, and away from me—and yet the seeing her from
time to time, and a word now and again, was a pleasure to
me, greater maybe than I confessed to myself—the greatest
that I had in life, indeed.'

She made no sign, and he continued, slowly and
watchfully, and still with that pale earnestness in his face.

'And then I wrote things about her—and amused myself with fancies—well, what harm could that do to her?—
so long as she knew nothing about it. And I thought I
was doing no harm to myself either, for I knew it was impossible there could be anything between us, and that she
would be going away sooner or later, and I too. Yes, and
I did go away, and in high feather, to be sure, and everything was to be for the best, and I was to have a fight for
money like the rest of them. God help me, lassie, before I
was a fortnight in the town, my heart was like to break.'

She sate quite still and silent, trembling a little, perhaps,
her eyes downcast, her fingers working nervously with the
edge of the small shawl she wore.

'I had cut myself away from the only thing I craved for
in the world—just the seeing and speaking to her from time
to time, for I had no right to think of more than that; and
I was alone and down-hearted; and I began to ask myself
what was the use of this slavery. Ay, there might have
been a use in it—if I could have said to myself, "Well,
now, fight as hard as ye can, and if ye win, who knows but
that ye might go back to the north, and claim her as the
prize?" But that was not to be thought of. She had
never hinted anything of the kind to me, nor I to her; but
when I found myself cut away from her like that, the days
were terrible, and my heart was like lead, and I knew that
I had cast away just everything that I cared to live for.

Then I fell in with some companions—a woman cousin o'
mine and some friends of hers—and they helped to make
me forget what I didna wish to think of, and so the time
passed. Well, now, that is the truth; and ye can understand, Miss Douglas, that I have no heart to begin again,
and the soldiering seemed the best thing for me, and a rifle-
bullet my best friend. But—but I will keep the promise
I made to ye—that is enough on that score; oh yes, I
will keep that promise, and any others ye may care to ask;
only I cannot bide in Glasgow.'

He heard a faint sob; he could see that tears were
gliding stealthily down her half-hidden face; and his heart
was hot with anger against himself that he had caused her
this pain. But how could he go away? A timid hand
sought his, and held it for a brief moment with a tremulous
clasp.

'I am very sorry, Ronald,' she managed to say, in a
broken voice. 'I suppose it could not have been otherwise—I suppose it could not have been otherwise.'

For some time they sate in silence—though he could
hear an occasional half-stifled sob. He could not pretend
to think that Meenie did not understand; and this was
her great pity for him; she did not drive him away in
anger—her heart was too gentle for that.

'Miss Douglas,' said he at length, 'I'm afraid I've
spoiled your walk for you wi' my idle story. Maybe the
best thing I can do now is just to leave you.'

'No—stay,' she said, under her breath; and she was
evidently trying to regain her composure. 'You spoke—
you spoke of that girl—O Ronald, I wish I had never
come to Glasgow!—I wish I had never heard what you
told me just now!'

And then, after a second—

'But how could I help it—when I heard what was happening to you, and all the wish in the world I had was to know that you were brave and well and successful and happy? I could not help it! . . . And now—and now— Ronald,' she said, as if with a struggle against that choking weight of sobs; for much was demanded of her at this moment; and her voice seemed powerless to utter all that her heart prompted her to say, 'if—if that girl you spoke of—if she was to see clearly what is best for her life and for yours—if she was to tell you to take up your work again, and work hard, and hard, and hard—and then, some day, it might be years after this, when you came back again to the north, you would find her still waiting?——'

'Meenie!'

He grasped her hand: his face was full of a bewilderment of hope—not joy, not triumph, but as if he hardly dared to believe what he had heard.

'O Ronald,' she said, in a kind of wild way,—and she turned her wet eyes towards him in full, unhesitating abandonment of affection and trust, nor could she withdraw the hand that he clasped so firmly,—'what will you think of me?—what will you think of me?—but surely there should be no hiding or false shame, and surely there is for you and for me in the world but the one end to hope for; and if not that—why, then, nothing. If you go away, if you have nothing to hope for, it will be the old misery back again, the old despair; and as for me—well, that is not of much matter. But, Ronald—Ronald—whatever happens—don't think too hardly of me—I know I should not have said so much—but it would just break my heart

to think you were left to yourself in Glasgow—with nothing
to care for or hope for——'

'Think of you!' he cried, and in a kind of wonder of
rapture he was regarding Meenie's tear-filled eyes, that
made no shame of meeting his look. 'I think of you—
and ever will—as the tenderest and kindest and truest-
hearted of women.' He had both her hands now; and he
held them close and warm. 'Even now—at this minute—
when you have given yourself to me—you have no thought
of yourself at all—it is all about me, that am not worth it,
and never was. Is there any other woman in the world so
brave and unselfish! Meenie, lass—no, for this once—
and no one will ever be able to take the memory away
from me—for this once let me call you my love and my
darling—my true-hearted love and darling!—well, now,
that's said and done with; and many a day to come I will
think over these few minutes, and think of sitting here
with you in this West End Park on the bench here, and
the trees around, and I will say to myself that I called
Meenie my love and my darling, and she was not angry—
not angry.'

'No, not angry, Ronald,' and there was a bit of a strange
and tender smile shining through the tears in the blue-gray
eyes.

'Ay, indeed,' said he, more gravely, 'that will be something for me; maybe, everything. I can scarcely believe
that this has just happened—my heart's in a flame, and
my head's gone daft, I think; and it seems as if there was
nothing for me but to thank God for having sent you into
the world and made you as unselfish and generous as you
are. But that's not the way of looking at it, my—my good
lass. You have too little thought for yourself. Why,

what a coward I should be if I did not ask you to think of the sacrifice you are making !'

'I am making no sacrifice, Ronald,' she said, simply and calmly. 'I spoke what my heart felt; and perhaps too readily. But I am going back to the Highlands. I shall stay there till you come for me, if ever you come for me. They spoke of my going for a while to my mother's cousins; but I shall not do that; no, I shall be at Inver-Mudal, or wherever my father is, and you will easily get to know that, Ronald. But if things go ill, and you do not come for me—or—or, if ye do not care to come for me—well, that is as the world goes, and no one can tell before-hand. Or many years may go by, and when you do come for me, Ronald, you may find me a gray-haired woman—but you will find me a single woman.'

She spoke quite calmly; this was no new resolve; it was his lips, not hers, that were tremulous, for a second or so. But only for a second; for now he was all anxiety to cheer her and comfort her as regards the future. He could not bring himself to ask her to consider again; the prize was too precious; rather he spoke of all the chances and hopes of life, and of the splendid future that she had placed before him. Now there was something worth striv-ing for—something worth the winning. And already, with the wild audacity that was now pulsating in his veins, he saw the way clear—a long way, perhaps, and tedious, but all filled with light and strewn with blossoms here or there (these were messages, or a look, or a smile, from Meenie), and at the end of it, waiting to welcome him, Love-Meenie, Rose-Meenie, with love-radiance shining in her eyes.

He almost talked her into cheerfulness (for she had

grown a little despondent after that first devotion of self-surrender) ; and by and by she rose from the bench. She was a little pale.

' I don't know whether I have done well or ill, Ronald,' she said, in a low voice, ' but I do not think I could have done otherwise. It is for you to show hereafter that I have done right.'

' But do you regret ?' he said quickly.

She turned to him with a strange smile on her face.

' Regret? No. I do not think I could have done otherwise. But it is for you to show to all of them that I have done right.'

' And if it could only be done all at once, Meenie ; that's where the soldier has his chance——'

' No, it is not to be done all at once,' she said ; ' it will be a hard and difficult waiting for you, and a slow waiting for me——'

' Do you think I care for any hardness or difficulty *now* ?' he said. ' Dear Meenie, you little know what a prize you have set before me. Why, now, here, every moment that I pass with you seems worth a year ; and yet I grudge every one——'

' But why ?' she said, looking up.

' I am going over to Pollokshaws the instant I leave you to try to pick up the threads of everything I had let slip. Dear lass, you have made every quarter of an hour in the day far too short ; I want twelve hours in the day to be with you, and other twelve to be at my work.'

' We must see each other very little, Ronald,' she said, as they set out to leave the Park. ' People would only talk——'

' But to-morrow——'

'No.   My sister is going down to Dunoon to-morrow to
see about the shutting up of the house for the winter, and
I am going with her.   But on Friday—if you were in the
Botanic Gardens—early in the forenoon—perhaps I could
see you then?'

'Yes, yes,' said he eagerly; and as they went down
towards the Woodland Road he strove to talk to her very
cheerfully and brightly indeed, for he could not but see
that she was a little troubled.

Then, when they were about to part, she seemed to try
to rouse herself a little, and to banish whatever doubts and
hesitations may have been harassing her mind.

'Ronald,' she said, with a bit of a smile, 'when you told
me of that girl in the Highlands that you knew, you said
you—you had never said anything to her that would lead
her to imagine you were thinking of her.   But you wrote
her a letter.'

'What?'

'Yes; and she saw it,' Meenie continued; but with
downcast eyes.   'It was not meant for her to see; but she
saw it.   It was some verses—very pretty they were—but
—but rather daring—considering that——'

'Bless me,' he exclaimed, 'did you see that?'

She nodded.   And then his mind went swiftly back to
that period.

'Meenie, that was the time you were angry with me.'

She looked up.

'And yet not so very angry, Ronald.'

'*But Love from Love towards school with heavy looks.*'
Not always.   Five miles an hour or so was the pace at
which Ronald sped over to Pollokshaws: and very much

astonished was the nervous little Mr. Weems over the new-found and anxious energy of his quondam pupil. Ronald remained all day there, and, indeed, did not leave the cottage until it was very late. As he walked back into the town all the world around him lay black and silent; no stars were visible; no crescent moon; nor any dim outline of cloud; but the dusky heavens were flushed with the red fires of the ironworks, as the flames shot fiercely up, and sent their sullen splendour across the startled night. And that, it may have' occurred to him, was as the lurid glare that had lit up his own life for a while, until the fires had gone down, and the world grown sombre and dead; but surely there was a clear dawn about to break by and by in the east—clear and silvery and luminous—like the first glow of the morn along the Clebrig slopes.

CHAPTER VII

AT THE PEAR-TREE WELL.

HE was almost glad that Meenie was going away for these two days, for he was desperately anxious to make up for the time he had lost; and the good-natured little Mr. Weems, instead of showing any annoyance or resentment, rather aided and abetted this furious zeal on the part of his pupil. All the same, Ronald found occasion to be within easy distance of the railway station on the morning of Meenie's departure; and about a few minutes to eight he saw herself and her sister step out of one of the cabs that were being driven up. If only he could have signalled a good-bye to her! But he kept discreetly in the background; glad enough to see that she was looking so fresh and bright and cheerful—even laughing she was, over some little mishap, as he imagined. And then so trim and neat she was in her travelling attire; and so daintily she walked—the graceful figure moving (as he thought) as if to a kind of music. The elder sister took the tickets; then they entered one of the carriages; and presently the train had slowly rolled away from the platform and was gone.

That glimpse of Meenie had filled his heart with un-utterable delight; he scarcely knew what he was doing when he got out into the open air again. The day seemed a festal day; there was gladness abroad in the very atmosphere; it was a day for good-companionship, and the drinking of healths, and the wishing of good wishes to all the world. His thoughts were all with Meenie—in that railway carriage flying away down to Greenock; and yet here, around him, there was gladness and happiness that seemed to demand some actual expression and recognition! Almost unconsciously—and with his brain busy with very distant matters—he walked into a public-house.

'Give me a glass of Highland whisky, my lad,' said he to the young man standing behind the counter: 'Talisker, if ye have it.'

The whisky was measured out and placed before him. He did not look at it. He was standing a little apart. And now Meenie would be out by Pollokshields, in the whiter air; by and by she would pass through Paisley's smoke; then through the placid pastoral country until she would come in sight of Dumbarton's castled crags and the long wide valley of the Clyde. And then the breezy waters of the Firth; and the big steamboat; and Meenie walking up and down the white deck, and drawing the sealskin coat a little tighter round the slight and graceful figure. There would be sunlight there; and fresh sea-winds blowing up from Arran and Bute, from Cumbrae and Cantire. And Meenie—

But at this moment his attention was somehow drawn to the counter, and he was startled into a consciousness of where he was and what he was doing. He glanced at the whisky—with a kind of shiver of fright.

'God forgive me—I did not want it,' he said to the astonished youth who was looking at him, 'but here's the money for 't.'

He put down the few coppers on the counter and hurriedly
left the place.   But the sudden fright was all.   As he sped
away out to Pollokshaws he was not haunted by any consciousness of having escaped from danger.   He was sure
enough of himself in that direction.   If a mortal craving
for drink had seized him, he would almost have been glad
of the fight ; it would be something to slay the dragon, for
Meenie's sake.   But he had naturally a sound and firm
constitution ; his dissipation had not lasted long enough
to destroy his strength of will ; and indeed this incident of
the public-house, so far from terrifying him with any doubts
as to the future, only served to remind him that dreams
and visions—and brains gone 'daft' with access of joy—
are not appropriate to the thoroughfares of a business city.

No ; as he walked rapidly away from the town, by way
of Strathbungo and Crossmyloof and Shawlands, what he
was chiefly busy with was the hammering out of some tune
that would fit the winter song he had chanced upon a few
days before.   And now he did not regard those gay and
galloping verses with a stupefied wonder as to how he ever
came to write them ; rather he tried to reach again to that
same pitch of light-heartedness ; and of course it was for
Meenie's delight, and for hers only, that this tune had to
be got at somehow.   It was a laughing, glad kind of a
tune that he wanted :

> *O then the warm west winds will blow,*
> *And all in the sunny weather*
> *It's over the moorlands we will go,*
> *You and I, my love, together.*
>
> Chorus : *And then the birds will begin to sing,*
> *And we will sing too, my dear,*
> *To give good welcoming to the spring,*
> *In the primrose-time o' the year—*

In the primrose-time,
In the primrose-time,
In the primrose-time o' the year—
To give good welcoming to the spring,
In the primrose-time o' the year.

Yes; and it was in the coming spring-time that he was to
try for the certificate in forestry; and thereafter—if he
were so fortunate as to get that—he might set forth on the
path that the Americans had so confidently sketched out
for him—the path that was now to lead him to Meenie, as
the final crown and prize. 'You may find me a gray-haired
woman, Ronald,' she had said, 'but you will find me a
single woman.' But still he was young in years; and there
was hope and courage in his veins; and what if he were to
win to her, after all, before there was a single streak of
middle age in the beautiful and abundant brown tresses?

Then, again, on the evening before the morning on
which he was to meet her in the Botanic Gardens, he
undid the package containing that anthology of verse
devoted to Meenie; and began to turn the pieces over,
wondering which, or if any of them, would please her, if
he took them to her. But this was rather a visionary
Meenie he found in these verses; not the real and actual
Meenie who had sate beside him on a bench in the West
End Park, and placed her hand in his, and pledged her
life to him, while the beautiful, tear-filled eyes sought his
so bravely. And could he not write something about this
actual Meenie; and about Glasgow; and the wonder she
had brought into the great, prosaic city? He tried his
hand at it, anyway, for a little while:

The dim red fires of yonder gleaming forge
Now dwell triumphant on the brow of night:

A thousand chimneys blackest smoke disgorge,
  Repelling from the world the stars' pale light :

A little taper shines adown the street,
  From out her casement where she lingers still
To listen to the sound of passing feet,
  That all the night with leaden echoes fill——

But he soon stopped. This was not like Meenie at all—
Meenie, who was ever associated in his mind with flowers
and birds and fair sunlight and the joy of the summer hills.
He threw that spoiled sheet into the fire ; and sought
among the old pieces for one that he might copy out fairly
for her ; and this is what he eventually chose :

All on a fair May morning
  The roses began to blow ;
Some of them tipped with crimson,
  Some of them tipped with snow.

But they looked the one to the other,
  And they looked adown the glen ;
They looked the one to the other,
  And they rubbed their eyes again.

' O there is the lark in the heavens,
  And the mavis sings in the tree :
And surely this is the summer,
  But Meenie we cannot see.

' Surely there must be summer
  Coming to this far clime ;
And has Meenie, Love Meenie, forgotten,
  Or have we mistaken the time?'

Then a foxglove spake to the roses :
  ' O hush you and cease your din ;
For I'm going back to my sleeping,
  Till Meenie brings summer in.'

Well, it was but a trifle ; but trifles are sometimes
important things when seen through lovers' eyes.

Next morning he went along to the Botanic Gardens; paid his sixpence with equanimity (for he had dispensed with the ceremony of dining the previous day) and entered. It was rather a pleasant morning; and at first sight he was rather shocked by the number of people—nursemaids and children, most of them—who were idly strolling along the trimly-kept walks or seated in front of the wide open par- terres. How was he to find Meenie in such a great place; and, if he did find her, were they to walk up and down before so many eyes? For he had guessed that Meenie would be in no hurry to tell her sister of what had happened —until the future seemed a little more clear and secure; it would be time enough to publish the news when that had assumed a more definite character.

But on and on he went—with glances that were keen and sharp enough—until suddenly, just as he had passed the greenhouses, he came almost face to face with Meenie, who was seated on a bench, all by herself, with a book before her. But she was not reading. 'O and proudly rose she up'; and yet shyly, too; and as he took her hand in his, the joy with which she regarded him needed no confes- sion in words—it was written there in the clear tender eyes.

'Indeed I am so glad to see you, Ronald!' she said. 'I have been so miserable these two days——'

'But why?' he asked.

'I don't know, hardly. I have been wondering whether I had done right; and then to go about with my sister, keeping this secret from her; and then I was thinking of the going away back to Inver-Mudal, and never seeing you, and not knowing how you were getting on. But now— now that you are here, it seems all quite right and safe.

You look as if you brought good news. What does he think, Ronald?'

'He?' he repeated. 'Who?'

''The old man out there at Pollokshaws, is it?'

Ronald laughed.

'Oh, the old gentleman seems pretty confident; but for very shame's sake I had to let him have a holiday to-day. I am not going over till to-morrow.'

'And he thinks you will pass?'

'He seems to think so.'

'I wish the time were here now, and that it was all well over,' she said. 'Oh, I should be so proud, Ronald; and it will be something to speak of to every one; and then— then that will be but the beginning; and day by day I shall be expecting to hear the news. But what a long, long time it seems to look forward to.'

'Ay, lass; and it will be worse for you than for me; for there will be the continual trying and hoping for me, and for you nothing but the weary waiting. Well——'

'Oh, but do you think I am afraid?' she said bravely. 'No. I have faith in you, Ronald. I know you will do your best.'

'I should deserve to be hanged and buried in a ditch if I did not,' said he. 'But we will leave all that for a while, Meenie; I want you to come for a stroll along the banks over the Kelvin. Would ye wonder to find some sea-gulls flying about?—they're there, though; or they were there a week or two ago. And do you know that I got a glimpse of you at the railway station on Wednesday morning?——'

'I did not see you, Ronald,' she said, with some surprise.

'No, no; I kept out o' the way. It's not for me, lass,

it's for you to say when any of your folk are to be told
what we are looking forward to; and for my part I would
as lief wait till I could put a clearer plan before them—
something definite.'

'And that is my opinion too, Ronald,' she answered, in
rather a low voice. 'Let it be merely an understanding
between you and me. I am content to wait.'

'Well, then,' said he, as they reached the top of the
high bank overhanging the river, and began to make their
way down the narrow little pathways cut through the trees
and shrubs, 'here is a confession: I was so glad to see
you on that morning—and so glad to see you looking so
well—that I half lost my senses, I think; I went away
through the streets in a kind o' dream; and, sure as I'm
here, I walked into a public-house and ordered a glass of
whisky——'

She looked up in sudden alarm.

'No, no, no,' said he contentedly, 'you need not fear
that, my good lassie; it was just that I was bewildered
with having seen ye, and thinking of where ye were going.
I walked out o' the place without touching it. Ay, and
what think ye o' Dunoon? And what kind of a day was
it when ye got out on the Firth?'

So she began to tell him of all her adventures and
experiences; and by this time they had got down near to
the water's edge; and here—of what value would his
knowledge of forestry have been otherwise?—he managed
to find a seat for her. They were quite alone here—the
brown river before them; several sea-gulls placidly paddling
on its surface, others flying and dipping overhead; and if
this bank of the stream was in shadow, the other—with
some small green meadows backed by clumps of elms and

maples—was bright and fair enough in the yellow autumn sunshine. They were in absolute silence, too, save for the continual soft murmur of the water, and the occasional whirring by of a blackbird seeking safety underneath a laurel bush.

'Meenie,' said he, putting one hand on her shoulder, 'here are some verses I copied out for ye last night— they're not much worth—but they were written a long time ago, when little did I think I should ever dare to put them into your hand.'

She read them; and there was a rose colour in her face as she did so : not that she was proud of their merit, but because of the revelation they contained.

'A long time ago?' she said, with averted eyes—but her heart was beating warmly.

'Oh,' he said, 'there are dozens and dozens of similar things, if ever ye care to look at them. It was many a happy morning on the hill, and many a quiet night at home, they gave me : but somehow, lass, now that I look at them, they hardly seem to grip ye fast enough. I want something that will bind ye closer to myself—something that ye can read when you are back in the Highlands—something that is known only to our two selves. Well, now, these things that I have written from time to time—you're a long way off in them somehow—the Meenie that's in them is, not this actual Meenie, warm and kind and generous and breathing——'

'And a little bit happy, Ronald, just at present,' she said, and she took his hand.

'And some day, when I get through with busier work, I must try to write you something for yourself——'

'But, Ronald, all these pieces you speak of belong to

me,' she said promptly, 'and I want them, every one—
every, every one. Yes, and I specially want that letter—
if you have not kept it, then you must remember it, and
write it out for me again——'

'I came across it last night,' said he, with an embarrassed
laugh. 'Indeed I don't wonder you were angry.'

'I have told you before, Ronald, that I was not angry,'
she said, with a touch of vexation. 'Perhaps I was a little
—a little frightened—and scarcely knowing how much you
meant——'

'Well, you know now, Meenie dear; but last night,
when I was going over those scraps of things, I can tell
you I was inclined to draw back. I kept saying to myself—"What! is she really going to see herself talked
about in this way?" For there's a good deal of love-making
in them, Meenie, and that's a fact; I knew I could say
what I liked, since no one would be any the wiser, but,
last night, when I looked at some of them, I said—
"No; I'm not going to provoke a quarrel with Meenie.
She would fling things about, as the American used
to say, if she saw all this audacious song-writing about
her."'

'I'll chance that quarrel, Ronald,' she answered to this,
'for I want every, every, every one of them; and you must
copy them all, for I am going to take them with me when
I leave Glasgow.'

'And, indeed,' said he, 'you'll understand them better
in the Highlands; for they're all about Ben Loyal, and the
Mudal, and Loch Naver, and Clebrig.'

'And to think you hid them from me all that time!'

'Why, Meenie darling, you would have called on the
whole population to drive me out of the place if I had

shown them to you. Think of the effect produced by a
single glance at one of them!—you tortured me for weeks
wondering how I had offended you.'

'Well, you can't offend me now, Ronald, *that way,*'
said she, very prettily.

And so their lovers' talk went on, until it was time for
Meenie to think of returning home. But just beyond these
Botanic Gardens, and down in a secluded nook by the side
of the river, there is a little spring that is variously known
as the Three-Tree Well and the Pear-Tree Well. It is a
limpid little stream, running into the Kelvin; it rises in a
tiny cavern and flows for a few yards through a cleft in the
rocks. Now these rocks, underneath the overarching trees,
have been worn quite smooth (except where they are scored
with names) by the footsteps of generation after generation
of lovers who, in obedience to an old and fond custom,
have come hither to plight their troth while joining hands
over the brooklet. Properly the two sweethearts, each
standing on one side, ought to join their hands on a Bible
as they vow their vows, and thereafter should break a sixpence in twain, each carrying away the half; but these
minor points are not necessary to the efficacy of this probably pagan rite. And so—supposing that Ronald had
heard of this place of sacred pilgrimage, and had indeed
discovered its whereabouts in his rambles around Glasgow
—and supposing him to have got a friendly under-gardener
to unlock a gate in the western palisades of the Gardens—
and then, if he were to ask Meenie to step down to the
river-side and walk along to the hallowed well? And yet
he made of it no solemn ceremony; the morning was
bright and clear around them; and Meenie was rather
inclined to smile at the curious old custom. But she went

through it nevertheless; and then he stept across the rill again; and said he—

'There's but this remaining now, Meenie darling—"Ae fond kiss and then we sever."'

She stepped back in affright.

'Ronald, not with that song on your lips! Don't you remember what it goes on to say?'

'Well, I don't,' he answered good-naturedly; for he had quoted the phrase at random.

'Why, don't you remember?—

> *" Had we never loved sae kindly,*
> *Had we never loved sae blindly,*
> *Never met—or never parted,*
> *We had ne'er been broken-hearted." '*

'My good-hearted lass,' said he, interlinking his arm with hers, 'ye must not be superstitious. What's in a song? There'll be no severance betwixt you and me—the Pear-Tree Well has settled that.'

'And that is not at all superstition?' said she, looking up with a smile—until she suddenly found her blushing face overshadowed.

CHAPTER VIII.

THE COMING OF TROUBLES.

THESE were halcyon days. Those two had arrived at a pretty accurate understanding of the times of each other's comings and goings; and if they could snatch but five minutes together, as he was on his way over to the south, well, that was something; and not unfrequently the lingering good-bye was lengthened out to a quarter of an hour; and then again when high fortune was in the ascendant, a whole golden hour was theirs—that was as precious as a year of life. For their hastily-snatched interviews the most convenient and secret rendezvous was Hill Street, Garnet Hill; a quiet little thoroughfare, too steep for cabs or carriages to ascend. And very cheerful and bright and pleasant this still neighbourhood looked on those October mornings; for there was yet some crisp and yellow foliage on the trees; and the little patches of green within the railings lay warm in the light; and on the northern side of the street the house-fronts were of a comfortable sunny gray. Ordinarily there were so few people about that these two could walk hand in hand, if they chose; or they could stand still, and converse face to face, when some more than usually interesting talk was going forward. And it was quite astonishing what a lot of things they had to say to each other, and the importance that attached to the very least of them.

But one piece of news that Meenie brought to these stolen interviews was by no means insignificant : she was now receiving marked attentions from a young Glasgow gentleman —attentions that her sister had perceived at a very early period, though Meenie had striven to remain blind to them. Nor was there anything very singular in this. Mr. Gemmill was exceedingly proud of his pretty sister-in-law; he had asked lots of people to the house for the very purpose of meeting her; she was the centre of interest and attraction at these numerous gatherings; and what more natural than that some susceptible youth should have his mind disturbed by an unwitting glance or two from those clear Highland eyes? And what rendered this prospect so pleasing to the Gemmills was this : the young man who had been stricken by these unintentional darts was no other than the only son of the founder of the firm in which Mr. Gemmill was a junior partner—the old gentleman having retired from the business some dozen years before, carrying with him a very substantial fortune indeed, to which this son was sole heir. In more ways than one this match, if it were to be a match, would be highly advantageous; and Mrs. Gemmill, while saying little, was secretly rejoiced to see everything going on so well. If Meenie chanced to ask what such and such a piece was (Mr. Frank Lauder played a little), even that slight expression of interest was inevitably followed by her receiving the sheet of music by post next morning. Flowers, again : one cannot very well refuse to accept flowers; they are not like other gifts; they may mean nothing. Then, it was quite remarkable how often he found himself going to the very same theatre or the very same concert that the Gemmills had arranged to take Meenie to ; and naturally—as it chanced he had no one going with him —he asked to be allowed to go with them.   He even talked of taking a seat in Maple Street Church (this was the church that the Gemmills attended), for he said that he was tired to death of the preaching of that old fogey, Dr. Teith, and that Mr. Smilie's last volume of poems (Mr. Smilie was the Maple Street Church minister) had aroused in him a great curiosity to hear his sermons.

And as for Mr. Frank Lauder himself—well, he was pretty much as other young Glasgow men of fashion ; though, to be sure, these form a race by themselves, and a very curious race too.   They are for the most part a good-natured set of lads ; free and generous in their ways ; not anything like the wild Lotharios which, amongst themselves, they profess to be ; well dressed ; a little lacking in repose of manner ; many of them given to boating and yachting —and some of them even expert seamen ; nearly all of them fond of airing a bit of Cockney slang picked up in a London music hall during a fortnight's visit to town.   But their most odd characteristic is an affectation of knowing-ness—as if they had read the book of nature and human nature through to the last chapter ; whereas these well-dressed, good-natured, but rather brainless young men are as innocently ignorant of that book as of most other books. Knowing but one language—and that imperfectly—is no doubt a bar to travel ; but surely nowhere else on the face of the globe could one find a set of young fellows—with similar opportunities set before them—content to remain so thoroughly untutored and untravelled ; and nowhere else a set of youths who, while professing to be men of the world, could show themselves so absolutely unversed in the

world's ways. But they (or some of them) understand the
lines of a yacht; and they don't drink champagne as sweet
as they used to do; and no doubt, as they grow into middle
age, they will throw aside the crude affectations of youth,
and assume a respectable gravity of manner, and eventually
become solid and substantial pillars of the Free, U.P., and
Established Churches.

This Frank Lauder was rather a favourable specimen of
his class; perhaps, in his extreme desire to ingratiate himself with Meenie, he assumed a modesty of demeanour that
was not quite natural to him. But his self-satisfied jocosity,
his mean interpretation of human motives, his familiarly
conventional opinions in all matters connected with the
arts, could not always be hidden beneath this mask of
meekness; and Meenie's shrewd eyes had discerned clearly
of what kind he was at a very early period of their acquaintance. For one thing, her solitary life in the Highlands
had made of her a diligent and extensive reader; while her
association with Ronald had taught her keen independence
of judgment; and she was almost ashamed to find how
absolutely unlettered this youth was, and how he would
feebly try to discover what her opinion was, in order to
express agreement with it. That was not Ronald's way.
Ronald took her sharply to task when she fell away from his
standard—or rather their conjoint standard—in some of
her small preferences. Even in music, of which this young
gentleman knew a little, his tastes were the tastes of the
mob.

'Why do you always get away from the room when
Mr. Lauder sits down to the piano?' her sister said, with
some touch of resentment.

'I can endure a little Offenbach,' she answered saucily,

'when I'm strong and in good health. But we get a little too much of it when he comes here.'

Of course Ronald was given to know of these visits and of their obvious aim; but he did not seem very deeply concerned.

'You know I can't help it, Ronald,' she said, one morning, as they were slowly climbing the steep little Randolph Terrace together, her hand resting on his arm. 'I can't tell him to go away while my sister keeps asking him to the house. They say that a girl can always show by her manner when any attention is displeasing to her. Well, that depends. I can't be downright rude—I am staying in my sister's house. And then, I wouldn't say he was conceited—I wouldn't say that, Ronald—but—but he is pretty well satisfied with himself; and perhaps not so sensitive about one's manner towards him as some might be. As for you, Ronald,' she said, with a laugh, 'I could send you flying, like a bolt from a bow, with a single look.'

'Could you, lass?' said he. 'I doubt it. Perhaps I would refuse to budge. I have got charge of you now.'

'Ah, well, I am not likely to try, I think,' she continued. 'But about this Mr. Lauder, Ronald—you see, he is a very important person in Mr. Gemmill's eyes; for he and his father have still some interest in the warehouse, I suppose; and I know he thinks it is time that Mr. Gemmill's name should be mentioned in the firm—not mere "Co." And that would please Agatha too; and so they're very polite to him; and they expect me to be very polite to him too. You see, Ronald, I can't tell him to go away until he says something—either to me or to Agatha; and he won't take a hint, though he must see that I would rather not have him send flowers and music and that; and then, again, I sometimes think it is not fair to you, Ronald, that I should allow anything of the kind to go on—merely through the difficulty of speaking——'

He stopped, and put his hand over the hand that lay on his arm : there was not a human being in sight.

'Tell me this, Meenie darling : does his coming to the house vex you and trouble you?'

'Oh no—not in the least,' said she, blithely and yet seriously. 'I am rather pleased when he comes to the house. When he is there of an evening, and I have the chance of sitting and looking at him, it makes me quite happy.'

This was rather a startling statement, and instantly she saw a quick, strange look in his eyes.

'But you don't understand, Ronald,' she said placidly, and without taking away her eyes from his. 'Every time I look at him I think of you, and it's the difference that makes me glad.'

Halcyon days indeed; and Glasgow became a radiant golden city in this happy autumn time; and each meeting was sweeter and dearer than its predecessor; and their twin lives seemed to be floating along together on a river of joy. With what a covetous care she treasured up each fragment of verse he brought her, and hid it away in a little thin leathern case she had herself made, so that she could wear it next her heart. He purchased for her little presents— such as he could afford—to show her that he was thinking of her on the days when they could not meet; and when she took these, and kissed them, it was not of their pecuniary value she was thinking. As for her, she had vast schemes as to what she was going to make for him when

she got back to the Highlands.   Here, in Glasgow, nothing
of the kind was possible.   Her sister's eyes were too sharp,
and her own time too much occupied.   Indeed, what between
the real lover, who was greedy of every moment she could
spare for these secret interviews, and the pseudo lover, who
kept the Queen's Crescent household in a constant turmoil
of engagements and entertainments and visits, Rose Meenie
found the hours sufficiently full ; and the days of her stay
in Glasgow were going by rapidly.

'But Scripture saith, an ending to all fine things must
be ;' and the ending, in this case, was the work of the
widow Menzies.   Kate felt herself at once aggrieved and
perplexed by Ronald's continued absence ; but she was even
more astonished when, on sending to make inquiries, she
found he had left his lodgings and gone elsewhere, leaving
no address.   She saw a purpose in this ; she leapt to the
conclusion that a woman had something to do with it ; and
in her jealous anger and mortification she determined on
leaving no stone unturned to discover his whereabouts.
But her two cronies, Laidlaw and old Jaap (the skipper
was away at sea again), seemed quite powerless to aid her.
They knew that Ronald occasionally used to go over to
Pollokshaws ; but further than that, nothing.   He never
came to the Harmony Club now; and not one of his former
companions knew anything about him.   Old Mr. Jaap
hoped that no harm had come to the lad, whom he liked ;
but Jimmy Laidlaw was none so sorry over this disappear-
ance : he might himself have a better chance with the widow,
now that Kate's handsome cousin was out of the way.

It was Kate herself who made the discovery, and that
in the simplest manner possible.   She and mother Paterson
had been away somewhere outside the town for a drive ;

and they were returning by the Great Western Road, one evening towards dusk, when all at once the widow caught sight of Ronald, at some distance off, and just as he was in the act of saying good-bye to a woman—to a young girl apparently. Kate pulled up the cob so suddenly that she nearly pitched her companion headlong into the street.

'What is it, Katie dear?'

She did not answer; she let the cob move forward a yard or two, so as to get the dog-cart close in by the pavement; and then she waited—watching with an eager scrutiny this figure that was now coming along. Meenie did not notice her; probably the girl was too busy with her own thoughts; but these could not have been sad ones, for the bright young face, with its tender colour rather heightened by the sharpness of the evening air, seemed happy enough.

'Flying high, he is,' was Kate Menzies's inward comment as she marked the smart costume and the well-bred air and carriage of this young lady.

And then, the moment she had passed, Kate said quickly—

'Here, auntie, take the reins, and wait here. Never mind how long. He'll no stir; if you're feared, bid a laddie stand by his head.'

'But what is't, Katie dear?'

She did not answer; she got down from the trap; and then, at first quickly, and afterwards more cautiously, she proceeded to follow the girl whom she had seen parting from Ronald. Nor had she far to go, as it turned out. Meenie left the main thoroughfare at Melrose Street—Kate Menzies keeping fairly close up to her now; and almost directly after was standing at the door of her sister's house in Queen's Crescent, waiting for the ringing of the bell to

be answered. It needed no profound detective skill on
the part of Mrs. Menzies to ascertain the number of the
house, so soon as the girl had gone inside ; and thereafter
she hurried back to the dog-cart, and got up, and continued
her driving.

'Well, that bangs Banagher !' she said, with a loud laugh,
as she smartly touched the cob with the whip. 'The Great
Western Road, of a' places in the world ! The Great
Western Road—and he goes off by the New City Road—
there's a place for twa lovers to forgather !

> "*We'll meet beside the dusky glen, on yon burn side,*
> *Where the bushes form a cosie den, on yon burn side.*"

But the Great Western Road—bless us a', and the laddie
used to write poetry !'

'But what is it, Katie ?'

'Why, it's Ronald and his lass, woman : didna ye see
them? Oh ay, he's carried his good looks to a braw
market—set her up wi' her velvet hat and her sealskin
coat, and living in Queen's Crescent forbye. Ay, ay, he's
ta'en his pigs to a braw market——'

'It's no possible, Katie dear !' exclaimed mother
Paterson, who affected to be very much shocked. 'Your
cousin Ronald wi' a sweetheart ?—and him so much in-
debted to you——'

'The twa canary birds !' she continued, with mirth that
sounded not quite real. 'But never a kiss at parting, wi' a'
they folk about. And that's why ye've been hiding yourself away, my lad ? But I jalouse that that braw young
leddy o' yours would laugh the other side of her mouth if
her friends were to find out her pranks.'

And indeed that was the thought that chiefly occupied
her mind during the rest of the drive home. Arrived there,

she called for the Post-Office Directory, and found that the name of the people living in that house in Queen's Crescent was Gemmill. She asked her cronies, when they turned up in the evening, who this Gemmill was; but neither of them knew. Accordingly, being left to her own resources, and without letting even mother Paterson know, she took a sheet of paper and wrote as follows—

'SIR—Who is the young lady in your house who keeps appointments with Ronald Strang, formerly of Inver-Mudal? Keep a better look-out. Yours, A Friend.'

And this she enclosed in an envelope, and directed it to Mr. Gemmill of such and such a number, Queen's Crescent, and herself took it to the post. It was a mere random shot, for she had nothing to go upon but her own sudden suspicions; but she was angry and hot-headed; and in no case, she considered, would this do any harm.

She succeeded far better than she could have expected. Mr. Gemmill handed the anonymous note to his wife with a brief laugh of derision. But Agatha (who knew more about Ronald Strang than he) looked startled. She would not say anything. She would not admit to her husband that this was anything but an idle piece of malice. Nevertheless, when Mr. Gemmill left for the city, she began to consider what she should do.

Unfortunately, as it happened that morning, Meenie just played into her sister's hand.

'Aggie dear, I am going along to Sauchiehall Street for some more of that crimson wool: can I bring you anything?'

'No, thank you,' she said; and then instantly it occurred to her that she would go out and follow her sister, just to see whether there might be any ground for this anonymous

warning. It certainly was a strange thing that any one
should know that Meenie and Ronald Strang were even
acquainted.

And at first—as she kept a shrewd eye on the girl, whom
she allowed to precede her by some distance—all seemed
to go well. Meenie looked neither to the right nor to the
left as she walked, with some quickness, along St. George's
Road towards Sauchiehall Street. When she reached the
wool shop and entered, Mrs. Gemmill's conscience smote
her—why should she have been so quick to harbour
suspicions of her own sister? But she would still watch
her on the homeward way—just to make sure.

When Meenie came out again from the shop she looked
at her watch; and it was clear that she was now quickening
her pace as she set forth. Why this hurry, Mrs. Gemmill
asked herself?—the girl was not so busy at home. But
the solution of the mystery was soon apparent. Meenie
arrived at the corner of Hill Street; gave one quick glance
up the quiet little thoroughfare; the next moment Mrs.
Gemmill recognised well enough—for she had seen him
once or twice in the Highlands—who this well-built,
straight-limbed young fellow was who was now coming
down the steep little street at such a swinging pace.
And Meenie went forward to meet him, with her face
upturned to his; and she put her hand on his arm quite
as if that were her familiar custom; and away these
two went—slowly, it is true, for the ascent was steep—and
clearly they were heeding not anything and not anybody
around.

Agatha turned away and went home; she had seen
enough. To say that she was deeply shocked would hardly
be true; for there are very few young women who have

not, at some time or other in their lives, made an innocent
little arrangement by which they might enjoy an unobserved
interview with the object of their choice ; and, if there are
any such extremely proper young persons, Agatha Gemmill
knew that she had not been in the category herself. But
she was resolved upon being both indignant and angry.
It was her duty. There was this girl wilfully throwing
away all the chances of her life. A gamekeeper !—that
her sister should be for marrying a gamekeeper just at the
time that Mr. Gemmill expected to have his name announced
as a partner in the great firm ! Nay, she made no doubt
that Meenie had come to Glasgow for the very purpose of
seeking him out. And what was to become of young
Frank Lauder ? Indeed, by the time Meenie returned
home, her sister had succeeded in nursing up a considerable volume of wrath ; for she considered she was doing
well to be angry.

But when the battle-royal did begin, it was at first all on
one side. Meenie did not seek to deny anything. She
quite calmly admitted that she meant to marry Ronald,
if ever their circumstances should be so favourable. She
even confessed that she had come to Glasgow in the hope
of seeing him. Had she no shame in making such an
avowal ?—no, she said, she had none ; none at all. And
what had she meant by encouraging Mr. Lauder ?—she
had not encouraged him in any way, she answered ; she
would rather have had none of his attentions.

But it was when the elder sister began to speak angrily
and contemptuously of Ronald that the younger sister's
eyes flashed fire and her lips grew pale.

' A gentleman ?' she retorted. ' I might marry a gentleman ? I tell you there is no such gentleman—in manner,

in disposition, in education—I say there is no such gentleman as he is comes to this house !'

' Deary me !' said Agatha sarcastically, but she was
rather frightened by this unwonted vehemence. ' To think
that a gamekeeper——'

'.He is not a gamekeeper ! He will never be a gamekeeper again. But if he were, what should I care? It was
as a gamekeeper that I learnt to know him. It was as a gamekeeper that I gave him my love. Do you think I care what
occupation he follows when I know what he is himself?'

'Hoity-toity! Here's romance in the nineteenth century!
—and from you, Meenie, that were always such a sensible
girl ! But I'll have nothing to do with it. Back you pack
to the Highlands, and at once ; that's what I have got to
say.'

' I am quite willing to go back,' the girl said proudly.

' Ah, because you think you will be allowed to write to
him ; and that all the fine courting will go on that way ;
and I've no doubt you're thinking he's going to make money
in Glasgow—for a girl as mad as you seem to be will
believe anything. Well, don't believe *that.* Don't believe
you will have any fine love-making in absence, and all that
kind of stuff. Mother will take good care. I should not
wonder if she sent you to a school in Germany, if the
expense were not too great—how would you like that ?'

' But she will not.'

' Why, then ?'

' Because I will not go.'

' Here's bravery ! I suppose you want something more
heroic—drowning yourself because of your lost love—or
locking yourself up in a convent to escape from your cruel
parents—something that will make the papers write things

about you?   But I think you will find a difference after you
have been two or three months at Inver-Mudal.   Perhaps
you will have come to your senses then.   Perhaps you will
have learnt what it was to have had a good prospect of
settling yourself in life—with a respectable well-conducted
young man—of good family—the Lauders of Craig themselves are not in the least ashamed that some of the family
have been in business—yes, you will think of that, and that
you threw the chance away because of an infatuation about
a drunken ne'er-do-weel——'

'He is not—he is not!' she said passionately; and her
cheeks were white; but there was something grasping her
heart, and like to suffocate her, so that she could not protest more.

'Anyway, I will take care that I shall have nothing to
do with it,' the elder sister continued; 'and if you should
see him again before you go, I would advise you to bid
him good-bye, for it will be the last time.   Mother will
take care of that, or I am mistaken.'

She left the room; and the girl remained alone—proud
and pale and rebellious; but still with this dreadful weight
upon her heart, of despair and fear that she would not
acknowledge.   If only she could see Ronald!   One word
from him—one look—would be enough.   But if this were
true?—if she were never to be allowed to hear from him
again?—they might even appeal to himself, and who could
say what promise they might not extract from him, if they
were sufficiently cunning of approach?   They might say it
was for her welfare—they might appeal to his honour—they
might win some pledge from him—and she knowing nothing
of it all!   If only she could see him for one moment!
The very pulses of her blood seemed to keep repeating his

name at every throb—yearning towards him, as it were;
and at last she threw herself down on the sofa and buried
her head in the cushion, and burst into a wild and long-
continued fit of weeping and sobbing.   But this in time
lightened the weight at her heart, at any rate; and when
at length she rose—with tear-stained cheeks and tremulous
lips and dishevelled hair—there was still something in her
look that showed that the courage with which she had
faced her sister was not altogether gone; and soon the lips
had less of tremulousness about them than of a proud
decision; and there was that in the very calmness of her
demeanour that would have warned all whom it might
concern that the days of her placid and obedient girlhood
were over.

CHAPTER IX.

NEVER was there a gayer party than this that was walking from the hotel towards the shores of Lake George, on a brilliant and blue-skied October morning. Perhaps the most demure—or the most professedly demure—was Miss Carry Hodson herself, who affected to walk apart a little; and swung carelessly the fur cape she carried in her hand; and refused all kinds of attentions from a tall, lank, long-haired young man who humbly followed her; and pretended that she was wholly engrossed with the air of

> *' I'm in love, sweet Mistress Prue,*
> *Sooth I can't conceal it ;*
> *My poor heart is broke in two—*
> *You alone can heal it.'*

As for the others of this light-hearted and laughing group of young folk, they were these : Miss Kerfoot, a fresh-coloured, plump, pleasant-looking girl, wearing much elaborate head-gear rather out of proportion to her stature ; her married sister, Mrs. Lalor, a grass-widow who was kind enough to play chaperon to the young people, but whose effective black eyes had a little trick of roving on their own account —perhaps merely in quest of a joke ; Dr. Thomas P. Tilley, an adolescent practitioner, who might have inspired a little more confidence in his patients had he condescended to

powder his profuse chestnut-brown hair; and, finally, the long
and lank gentleman who waited so humbly on Miss Hodson,
and who was Mr. J. C. Huysen, of the *Chicago Citizen.*
Miss Carry had at length—and after abundant meek inter-
cession and explanations and expressions of remorse—
pardoned the repentant editor for his treatment of Ronald.
It was none of his doing, he vowed and declared. It was
some young jackass whom the proprietors of the paper had
introduced to him. The article had slipped in without his
having seen it first. If only her Scotch friend would write
something more, he would undertake that the *Chicago
Citizen* would treat it with the greatest respect. And so
forth. Miss Carry was for a long time obdurate, and
affected to think that it was poetical jealousy on his part
(for the lank-haired editor had himself in former days written
and published sentimental verse—a fact which was not
forgotten by one or two of the wicked young men on the
staff of the *N. Y. Sun* when Mr. Huysen adventured into
the stormy arena of politics); but in the end she restored
him to favour, and found him more submissive than ever.
And in truth there was substantial reason for his submis-
sion. The *Chicago Citizen* paid well enough, no doubt;
but the editor of that journal had large views; and Miss
Hodson's husband—if all stories were true—would find
himself in a very enviable position indeed.

'Mayn't I carry your cape for you, Miss Hodson?' the
tall editor said, in the most pleading way in the world.

'No, I thank you,' she answered, civilly enough; but she
did not turn her head; and she made believe that her mind
was wholly set on

'I'm in love, sweet Mistress Prue,
Sooth I can't conceal it.'

This timid prayer and its repulse had not escaped the sharp observation of Miss Kerfoot.

'Oh,' said she, 'there's no doing anything with Carry, ever since we came to Fort George. Nothing's good enough for her; the hills are not high enough; and the place is not wild enough; and there's no catching of salmon in drenching rain—so there's no amusement for her. Amusement? I know where the trouble is; I know what amusement she wants; I know what makes her grumble at the big hotels, and the decent clothes that people prefer to wear, and the rattlesnakes, and all the rest. Of course this lake can't be like the Scotch lake; there isn't a handsome young gamekeeper here for her to flirt with. Flirtation, was it? Well, I suppose it was, and no more. I don't understand the manners and customs of savage nations. Look at her now. Look at that thing on her head. I've heard of girls wearing true-love knots, and rings, and things of that kind, to remind them of their sweethearts; but I never heard of their going about wearing a yellow Tam-o'- Shanter.'

Miss Carry smiled a superior smile; she would pay no heed to these ribald remarks; apparently she was wholly engrossed with

'I'm in love, sweet Mistress Prue.'

'It isn't fair of you to tell tales out of school, Em,' the young matron said.

'But I wasn't there. If I had been, there would have been a little better behaviour. Why, I never! Do you know how they teach girls to use a salmon-rod in that country?'

The question was addressed to Mr. Huysen; but Miss Kerfoot's eyes were fixed on Miss Carry.

'No, I don't,' he answered.

'Oh, you don't know,' she said. 'You don't know. Really. Well, I'll tell you. The gamekeeper—and the handsomer the better—stands overlooking the girl's shoulder; and she holds the rod; and he grips her hand and the rod at the same time.'

'But I know how,' the young Doctor interposed. 'See here—give me your hand—I'll show you in a minute.'

'Oh no, you shan't,' said she, instantly disengaging herself; 'this is a respectable country. We don't do such things in New York State. Of course, over there it's different. Oh yes; if I were there myself—and—and if the gamekeeper was handsome enough—and if he asked me to have a lesson in salmon-fishing—don't you think I would go? Why, I should smile!'

But here Miss Carry burst out laughing; for her friend had been caught. These two girls were in the habit of talking the direst slang between themselves (and occasionally Miss Carry practised a little of it on her papa), but this wickedness they did in secret; outsiders were not supposed to know anything of that. And now Dr. Tilley did not seem very much pleased at hearing Miss Kerfoot say 'I should smile'; and Miss Kerfoot looked self-conscious and amused and a little embarrassed; and Carry kept on laughing. However, it all blew over; for now they were down at the landing stage; and presently the Doctor was handing them into the spick and span new cat-boat that he had just had sent through from New York that autumn.

Indeed it was a right joyous party that now went sailing out on the clear lapping waters; for there was a brisk breeze blowing; and two pairs of sweethearts in one

small boat's cargo make a fair proportion; and Lake
George, in October, before the leaves are beginning to fall,
is just about as beautiful a place as any one can want.
The far low hills were all red and brown and yellow with
maple and scrub oak, except where the pines and the
hemlocks interposed a dark blue-green; and nearer at
hand, on the silvery surface of the lake, were innumerable
small wooded islands, with a line of white foam along
the windward shores; and overhead a perfectly cloudless
sky of intense and brilliant blue.   And if these were not
enough for the gay voyagers, then there were other things
—laughter, sarcasm, subtle compliments, daring or stolen
glances; until at last the full tide of joy burst into song.
Who can tell which of them it was that started

> ' *I'se gwine back to Dixie, no more I'se gwine to wander,*
> *My heart's turned back to Dixie, I can't stay here no longer*'?

No matter; nor was it of much consequence whether
the words of the song were of a highly intellectual cast, nor
whether the music was of the most distinguished character,
so long as there was a chorus admirably adapted for
soprano, alto, tenor, and bass.   It was very speedily clear
that this was not the first time these four had practised
the chorus (Mrs. Lalor was allowed to come in just where
she pleased), nor was there any great sadness in their
interpretation of the words—

Dix - ie, I'se gwine where the or - ange blos - soms grow, . . .

. . . For I hear the chil-dren call - ing, I see their sad tears

ad lib.

fall-ing, My heart's turn'd back to Dix - ie, And I must go.

colla voce.

It is impossible to say how often they repeated the chorus ; until Mrs. Lalor asked the girls why they were so fond of singing about orange blossoms, and then presently they turned to something else.

All this time they were beating up against a stiff but steady head-wind; the Doctor at the tiller; the lank editor standing by the mast at the bow; the girls and their chaperon snugly ensconced in the capacious cockpit, but still having to dodge the enormously long boom when the boat was put about. The women-folk, of course, paid no attention to the sailing; they never do; they were quite happy in leaving the whole responsibility on the owner of the craft; and were entirely wrapped up in their own petty affairs. Nay, so recklessly inconsiderate were they that they began to be angry because Dr. Tilley would not get out his banjo—which was in the tiny cabin, or rather locker, at the bow. They wanted to sing ' Dancing in the Barn,' they said. What was the use of that without a banjo to play the dance music?

'Very well,' said the complaisant Doctor, ' we'll run into some quiet creek in one of the islands; and then I'll see what I can do for you.'

No, no, they said; they wanted to sing sailing; they did not wish to go ashore, or near the shore. Well, the amiable Doctor scarce knew how to please them, for he could not steer the boat and play the banjo at the same time; and he was not sure about entrusting the safety of so precious a cargo to the uncertain seamanship of the editor. However, they were now a long way from Fort George; they might as well take a run back in that direction; and so—the boat having been let away from the wind and put on a fair course for the distant landing-stage—Mr. Huysen was called down from the bow and directed as to how he should steer; and then the Doctor went forward and got out the banjo.

Now this ' Dancing in the Barn ' (the words are idiotic enough) has a very catching air; and no sooner had the Doctor—who was standing up on the bit of a deck forward, where Jack Huysen had been—begun the tinkling prelude than the girls showed little movements of hands and feet, as if they were performing an imaginary ' cake-walk.'

' Oh, we'll meet at the ball in the evening,
Kase I love to pass the time away'

—they were all singing at it now; they did not wait for
any chorus; and Miss Carry had caught Miss Em's hand,
and was holding it on high, and keeping time to the music,
as if she were in reality leading her down the barn.

ge-ther, Kase now's the time for you to larn,   Ban-jos

ring-ing,   Nig-gers sing-ing,   And danc-ing in the barn.

Then came in the rippling dance—played as a solo on the
banjo; and so catching was it that the two girls stood up,
and made believe to dance a little. You see, the boat was
running free before the wind, and there was scarcely any
appreciable motion, though she was going at a good speed,
for her mainsail was enormously large and the breeze was
brisk.

'I say, Huysen,' the Doctor called, while he was
playing the dance, 'look what you're about. Never mind
the singing. Keep her bow straight for the landing-stage.'

Then the next verse began—

> *'Den we's off to work in de morning,*
> *Singing as we go out to de field,'*

and they all went at it with a will. And then the chorus;
and then the light rippling dance—

and the two girls were on their feet again, making believe
to posture a little, while the sharp clear notes of the banjo
tinkled and tinkled, amid the steady swishing noise of the
water along the side of the boat.   But all of a sudden there
was a startled cry of warning—the banjo was dropped on
the deck, and the Doctor sprung aft in a vain effort to
check what he had seen was coming; the next moment
the great boom came heavily swinging along, accelerating

its pace as it went out to leeward, until there was a frightful crash that seemed to tear the whole craft to pieces. And then, in this wild lurch, what had happened? Tilley was the first to see. There was something in the water. He tore off his coat and slipped over the boat's side—heeding nothing of the piercing screams of those he had left, but shaking the wet from his eyes and nose and mouth, and looking all around him like a Newfoundland dog. Then he caught sight of a small floating object—some dozen yards away—and he made for that: it was the yellow Tam-o'-Shanter, he could see; then he heard a half-stifled cry just behind him, and turning round was just able to catch hold of Carry Hodson before she sank a second time. However, she was quite passive—perhaps she had been stunned by a blow from the boom; and he was an excellent swimmer; and he could easily keep her afloat— if only Jack Huysen knew enough about sailing to get the boat back speedily. It was in vain to think of swimming with her to the shore; the land was too far off; and the weight of her wet clothes was increasing. He looked after the boat; it seemed a terrible distance away; but as far as he could make out—through the water that was blinding his eyes—they had got her round into the wind again and were no doubt trying to make for him.

Meanwhile, Jack Huysen had been so thunderstruck by what had occurred, when his own carelessness or an awkward gust of wind had caused the great boom to gybe, that for some seconds he seemed quite paralysed, and of course all this time the little craft was swinging along before the breeze. The shrieks of the women bewildered him, moreover. And then it occurred to him that he must get back—somehow, anyhow; and more by instinct than of

knowledge he jammed down the helm, and rounded the
boat into the wind, where the big sail began to flop about
with the loose mainsheet dragging this way and that.   And
then he set about trying little experiments—and in a
frantic nervousness all the same ; he knew, or he discovered,
that he must needs get in the mainsheet ; and eventually
the boat began to make uncertain progress—uncertain,
because he had been terrified, and was afraid to keep
proper way on her, so that she staggered up into the wind
incessantly.   But this at all events kept them near the
course they had come ; and from time to time she got
ahead a bit ; and the women had ceased their shrieking,
and had subsided, the one into a terrified silence, the
other into frantic weeping and clasping of her hands.

'Can't you—can't you look out ?   Why don't you look
out for them ?' he cried, though he scarce knew what he
said, so anxious was he about the tiller and those puffs of
wind that made the boat heel over whenever he allowed
the sail to fill.

And then there was a cry—from Mrs. Lalor.

'Look — look — this way — you're going away from
them.'

He could only judge by the direction of her gaze ; he
put the boat about.   She began to laugh, in a hysterical
fashion.

'Oh yes, yes, we are getting nearer—we are getting
nearer—he sees us—Em, Em, look !—poor Carry !—Oh,
quick, quick with the boat—quick, quick, quick !'

But the wringing of her hands was of little avail ; and
indeed when they did eventually draw cautiously close
to the two people in the water, the business of getting
them dragged on board proved a difficult and anxious

matter, for the girl was quite unconscious and lay in their hands like a corpse. The young Doctor was very much exhausted too; but at least he preserved his senses. He sat down for a minute to recover his breath.

'Jack,' he gasped, 'put my coat round her—wrap her warm—Mrs. Lalor, get off her boots and stockings—chafe her feet and hands—quick.'

And then he rose and went to where she was lying and stooped over her.

'Yes, yes, her heart is beating—come away with that coat, man.'

But it was his own coat that Jack Huysen had quickly taken off; and when Carry Hodson was wrapped in it, and when the women were doing what they could to restore her circulation, he fetched the other coat for the young Doctor, and made him put that on, though the latter declared he was all right now. And then the Doctor took the tiller, slacked out the mainsheet, and once more they were running before the wind towards Fort George. Not a word had been said about the cause of the mishap or its possible consequences.

These at first—and to Jack Huysen's inexpressible joy —seemed to be trivial enough. Immediately she had recovered consciousness she sate up, and began to say a few words—though with some difficulty; and indeed, so brave was she, and so determined to do something to relieve the obvious anxiety of these good friends of hers, that when at length they reached the landing-stage and got ashore she declared that she was quite recovered, that she could walk to the hotel as well as any of them, that she had never felt better in her born days. Nay, she made a joke of the whole matter, and of her heavy skirts, and of the possible contents of Jack Huysen's coat-pockets; and when they did reach the hotel, and when she had changed her wet garments, she came down again looking perfectly well —if a little bit tired.

It was not until the afternoon that she began to complain of shiverings; and then again, when dinner time arrived, Mrs. Lalor came down with the message that Carry had a slight headache, and would rather remain in her room. Next morning, too, she thought she would rather not get up; she had a slight cough, and her breathing was difficult; she had most relief when she lay quite still.

'What does this mean, Tom?' Jack Huysen said—and as if he feared the answer.

'I hope it means nothing at all,' was the reply; but the young Doctor looked grave, and moved away, as if he did not wish to have any further talking.

However, there was no perceptible change for the worse that day; and Miss Carry, when she could speak at all, said that she was doing very well, and implored them to go away on their usual excursions, and leave her to herself. A servant might sit outside in the passage, she said; if she wanted her, she could ring. Of course, this only sufficed to set Emma Kerfoot into a fit of weeping and sobbing —that Carry should think them capable of any such heartlessness.

But on the following morning matters were much more serious. She could hardly speak at all; and when she did manage to utter a few panting words she said it was a pain in her chest that was troubling her—not much; no, no, not much, she said; she wished they would all go away and amuse themselves; the pain would leave; she would be all right by and by.

'Jack, look here,' said the young Doctor, when they were together; 'I'm afraid this is pneumonia—and a sharp attack too.'

'Is it dangerous?' Huysen said quickly, and with rather a pale face.

The answer to this was another question;

'She left her mother at home, didn't she?'

'Yes,' said he breathlessly. 'Do you want to send for her? But that would be no use. Her mother could not travel just now; she's too much of an invalid; why, it was she who sent Carry away on this holiday.'

'Her father, then?'

'Why, yes, he's at home just now. Shall I telegraph for him?'

'No—not yet—I don't want to frighten her. We'll see in the morning.'

But long before the morning came they discovered how things were going with her. Late that night Mrs. Lalor, who had undertaken to sit up till her sister should come to relieve her, stole noiselessly along to the room of the latter and woke her.

'Em, darling, who is Ronald?' she whispered.

'Ronald? I don't know,' was the answer—for she was still somewhat confused.

'Carry is asking that one Ronald should be sent for—do come and see her, Em—I think she's wandering a little—she says there's never any luck in the boat except when Ronald is in it—I don't understand it at all——'

'But I do—I do now,' said the girl, as she hastily got up and put a dressing-gown and some wraps around her. 'And you'll have to send for the Doctor at once, Mary—he said he would not be in bed till two. She must be in a fever—that's delirium—if she thinks she is in the Highlands again.'

And delirium it was, though of no violent kind. No, she lay quite placidly; and it was only at times that she uttered a few indistinct words; but those around her now perceived that her brain had mixed up this Lake George with that other Scotch lake they had heard of, and they guessed that it was about salmon-fishing she was thinking when she said that it was Ronald that always brought good luck to the boat.

CHAPTER X.

A CHALLENGE.

ON the evening of the day on which Agatha Gemmill had made her portentous discovery about the secret interviews between her sister and Ronald, Mr. Gemmill—a little, red-headed man with shrewd blue eyes—came home in very good spirits.

'Look here, Aggie—here's an invitation for you,' he was beginning—when he saw that something was wrong. 'What is it now?' he asked.

And then the story was told him—and not without a touch of indignation in the telling. But Mr. Gemmill did not seem so horror-stricken as his wife had expected; she began to emphasise the various points; and was inclined to be angry with him for his coolness.

'Girls often have fancies like that—you know well enough, Agatha,' he said. 'All you have to do is to take a gentle way with her, and talk common sense to her, and it will be all right. If you make a row, you will only drive her into obstinacy. She will listen to reason; she's not a fool; if you take a quiet and gentle way with her——'

'A quiet and gentle way!' his wife exclaimed. 'I will take no way with her at all—not I! I'm not going to have any responsibility of the kind. Back she goes to the

Highlands at once—that's all the way I mean to take with her. See, there's a letter I've written to mother.'

'Then you mean to make a hash of this affair amongst you,' said he, with calm resignation. 'You will merely drive the girl into a corner; and her pride will keep her there——'

'Oh yes, men always think that women are so easily persuaded,' his wife broke in. 'Perhaps you would like to try arguing with her yourself? But, any way, I wash my hands of the whole matter. I shall have her packed off home at once.'

'I don't think you will,' the husband said quietly. 'I was going to tell you: the Lauders are giving a big dinner-party on the 27th—that is a fortnight hence; and here is an invitation for the three of us; and Frank Lauder as good as admitted this morning that the thing was got up for the very purpose of introducing Meenie to the old folk. Well, then, I have already written and accepted; and I will tell you this—I'm not going to offend the old gentleman just because you choose to quarrel with your sister.'

'Quarrel?' she retorted. 'Oh yes—she never can do any wrong. She has made a fool of you with her pretty eyes—as she does to every man that comes to the house. Why, they're like a set of great babies when she's in the room; and you would think from the way they go on that she was the Queen of Sheba—instead of the ill-tempered little brat she is.'

But Mrs. Gemmill was a sensible woman too.

'Of course we can't offend the old people. She'll have to stay. But as soon as that is over, off she goes to the Highlands again; and there she can stop until she has recovered her senses.'

However, this invitation was but an additional grievance. She went with it at once to Meenie's room.

'Look at that.   Read that.'

The girl glanced at the formal note—with no great interest.

'Do you know what that means?   That was meant to introduce you to Frank Lauder's family and friends.'

'I do not wish to go,' Meenie said perversely.

'But you'll have to go, for we have accepted for you. We can't offend and insult people simply because you are bent on making a fool of yourself.   But this is what I want to say: I had intended sending you back to Inver-Mudal at once ; but now you will have to stay with us another fortnight.   Very well, during that time I forbid you to have any communication with that man, of any kind whatever— do you hear ?'

She sate silent.

'Do you hear ?'

'Yes, I hear,' she said.

'Well ?'

'Very well.'

'But it is not very well,' the elder sister said angrily. 'I want to know what you mean to do.'

The answer was given with perfect calmness.

'I mean to do precisely as I have been doing.   I am not ashamed of anything I have done.'

'What ?   You are not ashamed ?   Do you mean to tell me that you will keep on meeting that man—in the public streets—making a spectacle of yourself in the streets of Glasgow—and bringing disgrace on yourself and your family ?'

'You are talking like a mad woman,' Meenie said proudly.

'You will see whether I act like one. I say you shall not be allowed to misconduct yourself while you are under this roof—that I will make sure of.'

'What will you do?' the girl said, in a strangely taunting tone: indeed, one could scarcely have believed that this was Meenie that was speaking. 'Lock me up in my room? They only do that in books. Besides, Mr. Gemmill would prevent your doing anything so ridiculous.'

'Oh, it's *he* that would come to let you out?' the elder sister said. 'You've discovered that, have you? What more, I wonder!'

But here the scene, which threatened to become more and more stormy, came to a sudden end. There was a sharp call from below—Mr. Gemmill having doubtless overheard some of these wild words.

'Agatha, come downstairs at once!'

So the girl was left once more alone—proud and pale and trembling a little, but with her mind more obdurate than ever. Nor would she go down to supper that night. Mr. Gemmill went twice to the door of her room (his wife would not budge a foot) and begged her to come downstairs. The first time she said she did not wish for any supper. The second time she said that if her conduct had been so disgraceful she was not fit to associate with his family. And so, being by nature a kindly-hearted man, he went away and got some food for her, and carried the little tray to her room with his own hands—a proceeding that only made his wife the angrier. Why should she be spoilt and petted with such foolish indulgence? Starvation was the best cure for her pride. But of course he was like the rest of the men—made simpletons of by a pair of girl's gray eyes.

Alas! all her pride and courage went from her in the

long dark hours of the night, and her sister's threats assumed a more definite and terrible meaning. It was true she had a fortnight's respite—during that fortnight she was her own mistress and could do as she pleased—but after? Would she be shut up in that little hamlet in the northern wilds, with absolutely no means of learning anything about Ronald, not permitted to mention his name, cut off from him as though he were in another world? She saw month after month go by—or year after year even—with no word or message coming to keep alive the fond hope in her breast. He might even be dead without her knowing. And how all too short this fortnight seemed, during which she might still have some chance of seeing him and gaining from him some assurance with regard to a future that looked more than ever uncertain and vague.

The next day it had been arranged between them that they were not to meet, for he was to be at home all that day and busy; but her anxiety was too great; she resolved to go to his lodgings and ask for him. She had never done that before; but now the crisis was too serious to let her heed what any one might say—indeed she did not think for a moment about it. So all the morning she went about the house, performing such small duties as had been entrusted to her, and wondering when the heavy rain would leave off. At last, about noon, when the dismal skies gave no sign of clearing, she got her ulster and deerstalker's cap, put on a thick pair of boots, and, armed with a stout umbrella, went out into the black and dripping world. No one had attempted to hinder her.

And yet it was with some curious sense of shame that she timidly rang the bell when she reached these obscure lodgings. The door was in a dusky entry; the landlady who answered the summons did not notice how the girl's cheeks were unusually flushed when she asked if Mr. Ronald Strang were at home.

'Yes, he is,' the woman said; and then she hesitated, apparently not quite knowing whether she should ask the young lady to step within or not.

'Will you tell him that I should like to see him for a moment—here!' she said.

In less than a minute Ronald was with her—and he had brought his cap in his hand; for he had guessed who this was; and instinctively he knew that he could not ask her to come within doors. But when she said she had something to say to him, and turned to face the dismal day outside, he could not but glance at the swimming pavements and the murky atmosphere.

'On such a morning, Meenie——'

'Oh, but I am well wrapped up,' she said, quite happily —for the mere sight of him had restored her courage, 'and you shall have the umbrella—yes—I insist—take it—well, then, I ask you to take it as a favour, for I am not going to have you get wet on my account.'

Of course he took the umbrella—to hold over her; and so they went out into the wet streets.

'I am so glad to see you, Ronald,' she said, looking up with a face that told its own story of joy and confidence; 'don't blame me; I have been miserable; I could not help coming to ask you for a little—a little comfort, I think, and hope——'

'But what have you been doing to your eyes, Meenie, darling? What kind of a look is that in them?'

'Well, I cried all last night—all the night through, I believe,' said she simply; but there was no more crying in her eyes, only light and love and gladness. 'And now, the moment I see you I think I must have been so foolish. The moment I see you everything seems right; I am no longer afraid; my heart is quite light and hopeful again.'

'Ay, and what has been frightening you, then?'

And then she told him all the story—as they walked along the wet pavements, with the bedraggled passers-by hurrying through the rain, and the tramway-cars and omnibuses and carts and cabs keeping up their unceasing roar. But Agatha's threats were no longer so terrible to her—now that she had hold of Ronald's arm; she glanced up at him from time to time with eyes full of courage and confidence; a single glimpse of him had driven away all these dire spectres and phantoms. Indeed, if the truth were known, it was he who was most inclined to take this news seriously; though, of course, he did not show that to her. No; he affected to laugh at the idea that they could be kept from communicating with each other; if she were to be sent back to Inver-Mudal, he said, that was only anticipating what must have happened in any case; it would no doubt be a pity to miss these few stolen minutes from time to time; but would not that be merely a spur to further and constant exertion?

'Ay, lass,' said he, 'if I could have any reasonable and fair prospect to put before them, I would just go to your friends at once; but all the wishing in the world, and all the work in the world, will not make next spring come any the quicker; and until I'm a certificated forester I'm loth to bother Lord Ailine, or anybody else, about a place. But what o' that? It's not a long time; and unless Mr. Weems is making a desperate fool o' me, I've a good

chance; and Lord Ailine will do his best for me among
his friends, that I know well.   In the meantime, if they will
not let you write to me——'

'But, Ronald, how can they help my writing to you, or
coming to see you, if I wish?'

'I was not thinking of your sister and her folk,' he
answered—and he spoke rather gravely.   'I was thinking
of your father and mother.   Well, it is not a nice thing for
a young lass to be in opposition to her own folk; it's a sore
trouble to both sides; and though she may be brave
enough at first, time will tell on her—especially when she
sees her own father and mother suffering through her
defiance of them.'

'Then I am not to write to you, Ronald, if they say no?'
she asked quickly, and with her face grown anxious again.

Well, it was a difficult question to answer off-hand;
and the noise in the streets bothered him; and he was
terribly troubled about Meenie having to walk through the
rain and mud.

'Will you do this for me, Meenie?' he said.   'I cannot
bear to have ye getting wet like this.   If we were to get
into an omnibus, now, and go down the town, I know a
restaurant where we could go in and have a comfortable
corner, and be able to talk in peace and quiet.   You and
I have never broken bread together, quite by ourselves.
Will you do that?'

She did not hesitate for a moment.

'Yes—if you think so—if you wish it,' she said.

And so they went down to the restaurant, which was
rather a big place, cut into small compartments; and one
of these they had to themselves, for it was but half-past
twelve as yet; and by and by a frugal little lunch was

before them. The novelty of the situation was so amusing —to Meenie at least—that for a time it drove graver thoughts away altogether. She acted as mistress of the feast; and would insist on his having this or that; and wondered that he had never even tasted Worcester sauce; and was altogether tenderly solicitous about him; whereas he, on the other hand, wished not to be bothered by any of these things, and wanted only to know what Meenie meant to do when she went back to Inver-Mudal.

'But you must tell me what you would have me do,' she said timidly.

'Well, I don't want you to quarrel with your mother and father on my account, and be living in constant wretchedness. If they say you are not to write to me, don't write——'

'But you said a little while ago there would be no difficulty in our hearing from each other,' she said, with wide open eyes.

'I have been thinking about it, good lass,' said he, 'and I don't want you to anger your folk and have a heavy heart in consequence. In the meantime you must look to them—you must do what they say. By and by it may be different; in the meantime I don't want you to get into trouble——'

'Then it's little you know how this will end, Ronald,' she said, rather sadly. 'I have thought over it more than you have. If I go back to Inver-Mudal prepared to do everything they wish me to do—I mean my mother, not my father, for I don't know what he might say—then it isn't only that you will never hear from me, and that I shall never hear a word from you; there's more than that: I shall never see you again in this world.'

He turned very pale ; and, scarcely knowing what he did, he stretched his hand over the narrow little table, and seized her hand, and held it firm.

'I will not let you go, then.   I will keep you here in Glasgow, with me, Meenie.   Do you think I can let you go away for ever?   For you are mine.   I don't care who says ay or no; you are mine; my own true-hearted girl ; the man or woman is not born that will sunder us two.'

Of course he had to speak in a low tone ; but the grip of his hand was sufficient emphasis.   And then he said, regarding her earnestly and yet half-hesitatingly —

'There is one way that would give you the right to judge what was best for yourself—that would give you the right to act or say what you pleased—even to leave your father's house, if that was necessary.   Will you become my wife, Meenie, before you go back to Inver-Mudal ?'

She started, as well she might ; but he held her hand firm.

'The thing is simple.   There is my brother the minister. We could walk over to his house, go through the ceremony in a few minutes, and you could go back to your sister's, and no one be a bit the wiser.   And then surely you would be less anxious about the future; and if you thought it right to send me a letter, you would be your own mistress as to that——'

'It's a terrible thing, Ronald!'

'I don't see that, Meenie, dear ; I've heard of more than one young couple taking their fate in their own hand that way.   And there's one thing about it—it " maks sikker. " '

They had some anxious talk over this sudden project—

he eager, she frightened—until the restaurant began to get crowded with its usual middle-day customers. Then Ronald paid his modest score, and they left; and now, as they made away for the western districts of the city, the day was clearing up somewhat, and at times a pale silvery gleam shone along the wet pavements. And still Meenie was undecided; and sometimes she would timidly steal a glance at him, as if to assure herself and gain courage; and sometimes she would wistfully look away along this busy Sauchiehall Street, as if her future and all the coming years were somehow at the end of it. As for him, now that he had hit upon this daring project, he was eager in defence of it; and urged her to give her consent there and then; and laboured to prove to her how much happier she would be at Inver-Mudal—no matter what silence or space of time might interpose between them—with the knowledge that this indissoluble bond united them. Meenie remained silent for the most part, with wistful eyes; but she clung to his arm as if for protection; and they did not hasten their steps on their homeward way.

When they parted she had neither said yes nor no; but she had promised to write to him that night, and let him know her decision. And in the morning, he got this brief message—the handwriting was not a little shaky, but he had scarcely time to notice that, so rapid was the glance he threw over the trembling lines :—

' DEAR RONALD—If it can be done quite, quite secretly —yes.   L. M.'

The signature, it may be explained, consisted of the initials of a pet name that he had bestowed on her. She

had found it first of all in some of those idle verses that he
now copied out for her from time to time ; and she had
asked him how he had dared to address her in that way,
while as yet they were but the merest acquaintances.   However, she did not seem very angry.

CHAPTER XI.

A WEDDING.

THIS golden-radiant city of Glasgow!—with its thousand thousand activities all awakening to join the noise and din of the joyous morning, and its over-arching skies full of a white light of hope and gladness and fair assurance of the future. The clerks and warehousemen were hurrying by to their desks and counters; work-folk were leisurely getting home for their well-earned breakfast; smart young men and slim-waisted women were already setting the shop windows to rights; great lorries were clattering their loads of long iron bars through the crowded streets; and omnibuses and tramway-cars and railway-trains were bringing in from all points of the compass their humming freight of eager human bees to this mighty and dusky hive. But dusky it did not appear to him, as he was speedily making his way across the town towards his brother's house. It was all transfigured and glorified — the interminable thoroughfares, the sky-piercing chimneys, the masses of warehouses, the overhead network of telegraph-lines, the red-funnelled steamers moving slowly away through the pale blue mist of the Broomielaw: all these were spectral in a strange kind of way, and yet beautiful; and he could not but think that the great mass of this busy multitude was well content with the pleasant

morning, and the nebulous pale-golden sunlight, and the
glimpses of long cirrus cloud hanging far above the city's
smoke.   For the moment he had ceased to hang his happiness on the chance of his succeeding with the Highland and
Agricultural Society.   Something far more important—and
wonderful—was about to happen.   He was about to secure
Meenie to himself for ever and ever.   Not a certificate in
forestry, but Meenie's marriage-lines—that was what would
be in his pocket soon !   And after ?—well, the long months, ·
or even years, might have to go by ; and she might be far
enough away from him, and condemned to silence—but
she would be his wife.

And then, just as he had reached the south side of the
river, he paused—paused abruptly, as if he had been struck.
For it had suddenly occurred to him that perhaps, after all,
this fine project was not feasible.   He had been all intent
on gaining Meenie's acquiescence ; and, having got that,
had thought of nothing but winning over the Reverend
Andrew into being an accomplice ; but now he was quickly
brought up by this unforeseen obstacle—could Meenie, not
being yet twenty-one, go through even this formal ceremony without the consent of her parents?   It seemed to
him that she could not—from his reading of books.   He
knew nothing of the marriage law of Scotland ; but it appeared to him, from what he could recollect of his reading,
that a girl under twenty-one could not marry without her
parents' consent.   And this was but the letting in of waters.
There were all kinds of other things—the necessity of having
lived a certain time in this or that parish ; the proclamation
of banns—which would be merely an invitation to her rela-
tives to interfere ; and so on.   He resumed his walk ; but
with less of gay assurance.   He could only endeavour to

fortify himself with the reflection that in the one or two instances of which he had heard of this very thing being done the young people had been completely successful and had kept their secret until they judged the time fitting for the disclosing of it.

When he reached his brother's house, the Reverend Andrew was in his study, engaged in the composition of the following Sunday's sermon; he was seated at a little table near the fire; a pot of tea on the chimney-piece; a large Bible and Cruden's Concordance lying open on the sofa beside him. The heavy, bilious-hued man rose leisurely, and rubbed his purplish hands, and put them underneath his coat-tails, as he turned his back to the fire, and stood on the hearth-rug, regarding his brother.

'Well, Ronald, lad, ye're not frightened for a cold morning, to come out with a jacket like that.'

'The morning's well enough,' said Ronald briefly; and forthwith he laid before his brother the errand on which he had come, and besought his assistance, if that were practicable. He told the story simply and concisely; not pleading any justification; but rather leaving the facts to speak for themselves. And would his brother help?—in other words, supposing there were no other obstacle in the way, would Andrew perform this ceremony for them, and so render their future proof against all contingencies? He was not asked for any advice; he was not asked to assume any responsibility; would he merely exercise this clerical function of his on their behalf—seeing how urgent matters were?

The Reverend Andrew was very much puzzled, not to say perturbed. He began to walk up and down the room; his head bent forward, his hands still underneath his coat-tails.

'You put me in a box, Ronald, and that's a fact,' said
he. 'I'm thinking my wishes as a brother will be for setting themselves up against my duty as a minister of the
Gospel. For I dare not counsel any young girl to defy the
authority of her own people——'

'She has not asked you for any counsel,' Ronald said
curtly. 'And besides we don't know what the authority
might be. I dare say, if her father knew all the circumstances, he would be on our side ; and I suppose he has as
much right to speak as her little spitfire of a mother.'

This was hard on Mrs. Douglas, who had always treated
Ronald with courtesy—if of a lofty and distant kind ; but
impetuous young people, when their own interests are at
stake, are seldom just to their elders. However, the Reverend Andrew now began to say that, if he were altogether an outsider, nothing would give him greater pleasure
than to see this wish of his brother's accomplished. He
had observed much, he said ; he had heard more ; he
knew the saving influence that this girl had exercised on
Ronald's life ; he could pray for nothing better than that
these two should be joined in lawful bonds, towards the
strengthening of each other, and the establishment of a
mutual hope and trust.

'But it would never do for me to be mixed up in it,
Ronald,' he continued. 'When it came to be known, think
of what ill-minded folk might say. I must have regard to
my congregation as well as to myself; and what if they
were to accuse me of taking part in a conspiracy ?'

'A conspiracy ?' Ronald repeated sharply. 'What
kind of a conspiracy ? To steal away a rich heiress—is
that it ? God bless me, the lass has nothing beyond what
she stands up in ! There's the sealskin coat Glengask gave

her; they can have that back, and welcome. What conspiracy would ye make out?'

'No, no, lad; I'm thinking what ill tongues might say.'

'Let them lick their own venom till they rot! What care I?'

'Yes, yes, yes, lad; but ye're not a placed minister; ye've but yourself and her to think of. Now, just wait a bit.'

He had gone back to his chair by the fire, and was seated there, staring into the red coals.

'I suppose you've heard of Dugald Mannering, of Airdrie?' he said, at length.

'Yes, indeed,' was the answer. 'Meenie—that is—Miss Douglas and I went to hear him the Sunday before last, but there was not a seat to be got anywhere—no, nor standing-room either.'

This Mr. Mannering was a young divine of the U.P. Church who had an extraordinary popularity at this time among the young people of the south of Scotland, and especially the young people of Glasgow, and that from a variety of causes. He was a singularly eloquent preacher—flowing, ornate, and poetical; he was entirely unconventional, not to say daring, in his choice of subjects; his quotations were as commonly from Shakespeare and Coleridge and Byron and Browning as from the usual pulpit authorities; he was exceedingly handsome, and rather delicate-looking — pale and large-eyed and long-haired; and he had refused the most flattering offers—'calls' is the proper word—from various west-end congregations of Glasgow, because he considered it his duty to remain among the mining-folk of Airdrie. When he did accept an invitation to preach in this or that city church, the young people from far and near came flocking to hear him; and a good many of their elders too, though these were not without certain prickings of conscience as to the propriety of devoting the Lord's day to what was remarkably like a revel in pure literature.

'Dugald's coming over here this afternoon,' the elder brother continued, as if he were communing with himself. 'He's an enthusiastic kind of fellow—he'll stick at nothing, if he thinks it's right. I wish, now, I had that portrait—but Maggie's away to school by this time——'

'What portrait?' Ronald asked.

The Reverend Andrew did not answer, but rose, and slowly and thoughtfully left the room. When he came back he had in his hand a photograph of Meenie framed in a little frame of crimson velvet, and that he put on the table: Ronald recognised it swiftly enough.

'He has got an eye for a handsome young lass, has Dugald,' the minister said shrewdly. 'I'll just have that lying about, as it were. Ay, it's a straightforward, frank face, that; and one that has nothing to hide. I'll just have it lying about when Dugald comes over this afternoon, and see if he doesna pick it up and have a good look at it.'

'But what mean ye, Andrew?' his brother said.

'Why, then, lad, I think I'll just tell Dugald the whole story; and if he's not as hot-headed as any of ye to carry the thing through, I'll be surprised. And I suppose if he marries ye, that's just as good as any one else?—for to tell you the truth, Ronald, I would rather not be mixed up in it myself.'

'And the banns?' said Ronald quickly. 'And the length of time in the parish? And the consent of her mother and father?'

The minister waved his hand with a superior air; these were trivial things, not to say popular errors; what had been of real consequence was the extent to which he dared implicate himself.

'I will not say,' he observed slowly, 'that I might not, in other circumstances, have preferred the publication of banns. It would have been more in order, and more seemly; for I do not like the interference of the secular arm in what should be a solely sacred office. Besides that, there is even a premium put on publicity, as is right; five shillings for the one proclamation, but only half-a-crown if you have them proclaimed two following Sundays. Well, well, we mustn't complain; I see sufficient reason; from all I can learn—and you were ever a truth-teller, Ronald, in season and out of season, as well I mind—it seems to me you are fulfilling the laws of God, and breaking none of man's making; so just you go to the Registrar of the parish, and give him the particulars, and deposit a half-crown as the worthy man's fee, and then, eight days hence, you call on him again, and he'll give you a certificate entitling you to be married in any house or church in the Kingdom of Scotland. And if there's no other place handy, ye're welcome to the room you're standing in at this minute; though I would as lief have the marriage take place anywhere else, and that's the truth, Ronald; for although I can defend what little I have done to my own conscience, I'm no sure I should like to stand against the clishmaclavers of a lot of old wives.'

'Where am I to find the Registrar, Andrew?' he asked: he was a little bewildered by the rapidity with which this crisis seemed approaching.

'I suppose you've a good Scotch tongue in your head,

and can ask for the loan of a Directory,' was the laconic answer. The Reverend Andrew had taken up the photograph again, and was regarding it. 'An honest, sweet face; as pretty a lass as ever a man was asked to work and strive for and to win. Well, I do not wonder, Ronald, lad—with such a prize before you—— But off you go now, for I must get to my work again; and if you come over and have a cup of tea in the afternoon, between four and five, I suppose Dugald Mannering will be here, and maybe ye'll be the best hand to explain the whole situation of affairs.'

And so Ronald left to seek out the Registrar; and as he went away through the busy and sunlit streets, he was asking himself if there was not one of all those people who could guess the secret that he carried with him in his bosom, and that kept his heart warm there.

The Rev. Dugald Mannering, as it turned out, was not nearly so eager and enthusiastic as Ronald's brother had prophesied; for it behoves a youthful divine to maintain a serious and deliberative countenance, when weighty matters are put before him for judgment. But afterwards, when the two young men were together walking away home through the dusky streets of Glasgow, the U.P. minister became much more frank and friendly and communicative.

'I see your brother's position well enough, Mr. Strang,' said he. 'I can understand his diffidence; and it is but right that he should be anxious not to give the envious and ill-natured a chance of talking. He is willing to let the ceremony take place in his house, because you are his brother. If I were you, I would rather have it take place anywhere else —both as being fairer to him, and as being more likely to ensure secrecy, which you seem to think necessary.'

Ronald's face burned red : should he have to ask Meenie to come to his humble lodgings, with the wondering, and perhaps discontented and suspicious, landlady, as sole onlooker?

'Well, now,' the young preacher continued, 'when I come to Glasgow, there are two old maiden aunts of mine who are good enough to put me up. They live in Rose Street, Garnethill ; and they're very kind old people. Now I shouldn't wonder at all if they took it into their head to befriend the young lady on this occasion—I mean, if you will allow me to mention the circumstances to them ; indeed, I am sure they would ; probably they would be delighted ; indeed I can imagine their experiencing a fearful joy on finding this piece of romance suddenly tumbling into the middle of their prim and methodical lives. The dear old creatures !—I will answer for them. I will talk to them as soon as I get home now. And do you think you could persuade Miss Douglas to call on them ?'

Ronald hesitated.

' If they were to send her a message, perhaps——'

' When are you likely to see her ?'

' To-morrow morning, at eleven,' he said promptly.

' Very well. I will get one of the old ladies to write a little note to Miss Douglas; and I will post it to you to-night; and to-morrow morning, if she is so inclined, bring her along and introduce yourself and her—will you ? I shall be there, so there won't be any awkwardness ; and I would not hurry you, but I've to get back to Airdrie to-morrow afternoon. Is it a bargain ?'

' So far as I am concerned—yes ; and many thanks to ye,' Ronald said, as he bade his companion good-bye and went away home to his solitary lodgings.

But when, the next morning, in Randolph Terrace—and
after he had rapidly told her all that had happened—he
suggested that she should there and then go along and call
on the Misses Mannering, Meenie started back in a kind of
fright, and a flush of embarrassment overspread her face.
And why—why—he asked, in wonder.

'Oh, Ronald,' she said, glancing hurriedly at her costume,
'these—these are the first of your friends you have asked me
to go to see, and do you think I could go like *this?*'

'*This*' meant that she had on a plain and serviceable
ulster, a smart little hat with a ptarmigan's wing on it,
a pair of not over-new gloves, and so forth.   Ronald
was amazed.   He considered that Meenie was always a
wonder of neatness and symmetry, no matter how she was
attired.   And to think that any one might find fault with
her !

'Besides, they're not my friends,' he exclaimed.   'I
never saw them in my life.'

'They know who your brother is,' she said.   'Do you
think I would give any one occasion to say you were marrying a slattern?   Just look.'

She held out her hands; the gloves were certainly
worn.

'Take them off, and show them the prettiest-shaped
hands in Glasgow town,' said he.

'And my hair—I know it is all rough and untidy--isn't
it now?' she said, feeling about the rim of her hat.

'Well, it is a little,' he confessed, 'only it's far prettier
that way than any other.'

'Ronald,' she pleaded, 'some other time—on Friday
morning—will Friday morning do?'

'Oh, I know what you want,' said he.   'You want to

go and get on your sealskin coat and your velvet hat and a
new pair of gloves and all the rest ; and do you know what
the old ladies are like to say when they see you ?—they'll
say, " Here's a swell young madam to be thinking of marrying a man that may have but a couple o' pounds a week or
so at first to keep house on." '

' Oh, will they think that ?' she said quickly. ' Well, I'll
—I'll go now, Ronald—but please make my hair smooth
behind—and is my collar all right ? '

And yet it was not such a very dreadful interview, after
all ; for the two old dames made a mighty fuss over this
pretty young creature ; and vied with each other in petting
her, and cheering her, and counselling her ; and when the
great event was spoken of in which they also were to play
a part they affected to talk in a lower tone of voice, as if it
were something mysterious and tragic and demanding the
greatest caution and circumspection. As for the young
minister, he sate rather apart, and allowed his large soft eyes
to dwell upon Meenie, with something of wistfulness in his
look.   He could do so with impunity, in truth, for the old
ladies entirely monopolised her. They patted her on the
shoulder, to give her courage ; they spoke as if they themselves had gone through the wedding ceremony a hundred
times. Was she sure she would rather have no other wit-
nesses ? Would she stand up at the head of the room
now, and they would show her all she would have to do ?
And they stroked her hand ; and purred about her ; and
were mysteriously elated over their share in this romantic
business ; insomuch that they altogether forgot Ronald—
who was left to talk politics with the absent-eyed young
parson.

Between this interview and the formal wedding a whole

week had to elapse ; and during that time Agatha Gemmill
saw fit to deal in quite a different way with her sister.   She
was trying reason now, and persuasion, and entreaty ; and
that at least was more agreeable to Meenie than being
driven into a position of angry antagonism.   Moreover,
Meenie did not seek to vaunt her self-will and independence too openly.   Her meetings with Ronald were few ;
and she made no ostentatious parade of them.   She was
civil to Mr. Frank Lauder when he came to the house.
Indeed, Mr. Gemmill, who arrogated to himself the success
of this milder method of treating the girl, was bold enough
to declare that everything was going on well ; Meenie had
as much common sense as most folk ; she was not likely
to throw herself away ; and when once she had seen old
Mr. Lauder's spacious mansion, and picture galleries, and
what not, and observed the style in which the family lived,
he made do doubt but that they would soon have to welcome Frank Lauder as a brother-in-law.

Trembling, flushed at times, and pale at others, and
clinging nervously to Ronald's arm, Meenie made her way
up this cold stone staircase in Garnethill, and breathless
and agitated she stood on the landing, while he rang the
bell.

'Oh, Ronald, I hope I am doing right,' she murmured.

'We will let the future be the judge of that, my good
girl,' he said, with modest confidence.

The old dames almost smothered her with their attentions and kindness ; and they had a bouquet for her—all
in white, as became a bride ; and they had prepared other
little nick-nacks for her adornment, so that they had to
carry her off to their own room, for the donning of these.
And when they brought her back—rose-red she was, and

timid, and trembling—each of them had one of her hands,
as if she was to be their gift to give away; and very important and mysterious were they about the shutting of the
doors, and the conducting the conversation in whispers.
Then the minister came forward, and showed them with
a little gesture of his hand where they should stand before
him.

The ceremonial of a Scotch wedding is of the simplest;
but the address to the young people thus entering life
together may be just anything you please. And in truth
there was a good deal more of poetry than of theology in
these mellifluent sentences of the Rev. Mr. Mannering's, as
he spoke of the obligations incurred by two young folk
separating themselves from all others and resolved upon
going through the world's joys and sorrows always side by
side; and the old dames were much affected; and when
he went on to quote the verses

> ' *And on her lover's arm she leant,*
> *And round her waist she felt it fold,*
> *And far across the hills they went*
> *In that new world which is the old,*'

they never thought of asking whether the lines were quite
apposite; they were sobbing unaffectedly and profusely;
and Meenie's eyes were rather wet too.   And then, when it
was all over, they caught her to their arms as if she had
been their own; and would lead her to the sofa, and over-
whelm her with all kinds of little attentions and caresses.
Cake and wine, too—of course she must have some cake
and wine!

'Should I, Ronald?' she said, looking up, with her eyes
all wet and shining and laughing: it was her first appeal to
the authority of her husband.

' As you like—as you like, surely.'

But when they came to him he gently refused.

' Not on your wedding day ! ' the old ladies exclaimed—
and then he raised the glass to his lips ; and they did not
notice that he had not touched it when he put it down
again.

And so these two were married now—whatever the
future might have in store for them ; and in a brief space
of time—as soon, indeed, as she could tear herself away
from these kind friends, she had dispossessed herself of
her little bits of bridal finery ; and had bade a long and
lingering good-bye to Ronald ; and was stealing back to
her sister's house.

CHAPTER XII

IN DARKENED WAYS.

IT was with feelings not to be envied that Jack Huysen stalked up and down the verandah in front of this Fort George hotel, or haunted the long, echoing corridors, eager to question any one who had access to the sick room. All the mischief seemed to be of his doing; all the help and counsel and direction in this time of distress seemed to be afforded by his friend Tilley. It was he—that is, Huysen —whose carelessness had led to the boating catastrophe; it was the young Doctor who had plunged into the lake and saved Carry's life. Not only that, but it was on his shoulders that there now seemed to rest the burden of saving her a second time; for she had gone from bad to worse; the fever had increased rapidly; and while Doctor Tilley was here, there, and everywhere in his quiet but persistent activity, taking elaborate precautions about the temperature of the room, instructing the two trained nurses whom he had telegraphed for from New York, and pacifying the mental vagaries of the patient as best he might, what could Jack Huysen do but wander about like an uneasy spirit, accusing himself of having wrought all this evil, and desperately conscious that he could be of no use whatever in mitigating its results.

She was not always delirious. For the most part she lay moaning slightly, breathing with the greatest difficulty, and complaining of that constant pain in her chest; while her high pulse and temperature told how the fever was rather gaining upon her than abating. But then again, at times, her face would grow flushed; and the beautiful soft black eyes would grow strangely bright; and she would talk in panting whispers, in an eager kind of way, and as if she had some secret to tell. And always the same delusion occupied her mind—that this was Loch Naver; that they had got into trouble somehow, because Ronald was not in the boat; that they had sent for Ronald, but he had gone away; and so forth. And sometimes she uttered bitter reproaches; Ronald had been ill-treated by some one; nay, she herself had been to blame; and who was to make up to him for what he had suffered at her hands?

'Not that he cared,' she said, rather proudly and contemptuously, one hushed evening that the Doctor was trying to soothe her into quietude. 'No, no. Ronald care what a conceited scribbling schoolboy said about him? No! I should think not. Perhaps he never knew—indeed, I think he never knew. He never knew that all our friends in Chicago were asked to look on and see him lectured, and patronised, and examined. Oh! so clever the news-paper-writer was—with his airs of criticism and patronage! But the coward that he was—the coward—to strike in the dark—to sit in his little den and strike in the dark! Why didn't Jack Huysen drag him out? Why didn't he make him sign his name, that we could tell who this was with his braggart airs? The coward! Why, Ronald would have felled him! No! no! He would not have looked the way the poor pretentious fool was going. He would have laughed. Doctor, do you know who he was? Did you ever meet him?'

'But who, Miss Carry?' he said, as he patted her hot hand.

She looked at him wonderingly.

'Why, don't you know? Did you never hear? The miserable creature that was allowed to speak ill of our Ronald. Ah! do you think I have forgotten? Does Jack Huysen think I have forgotten? No, I will not forget—you can tell him, I will not forget—I will not forget—I will not forget—'

She was growing more and more vehement; and to pacify her he had to assure her that he himself would see this matter put straight; and that it was all right, and that ample amends would be made.

Of course, he paid no great attention to these delirious wanderings; but that same evening, when he had gone into the smoking-room to report to Jack Huysen how things were going, this complaint of Miss Carry's happened to recur to his mind.

'Look here, Jack, what's this that she's always talking about—seems to worry her a good deal—some newspaper article—and you're mixed up in it, too—something you appear to have said or done about that fellow her father took such a fancy for—I mean, when they were in Scotland——'

'Oh, I know,' said the editor, and he blushed to the very roots of his long-flowing hair. 'I know. But it's an old story. It's all forgotten now.'

'Well, it is not,' the young Doctor said 'and that's the fact. She worries about it continually. Very strange, now,

how her mind just happened to take that bent. I don't
remember that we were talking much about the Scotch
Highlands. But they must have been in her head when
she fell ill; and now it's nothing else. Well, what is it
about the newspaper article, anyway?'

'Why, nothing to make a fuss about,' Jack Huysen said,
but rather uneasily. 'I thought it was all forgotten. She
said as much. Wonder you don't remember the article—
suppose you missed it—but it was about this same Highland fellow, and some verses of his—it was young Regan
wrote it—confound him, I'd have kicked him into Lake
Michigan before I let him write a line in the paper, if I'd
have known there was going to be this trouble about it.
And I don't think now there was much to find fault with—
I only glanced over it before sending it to her, and it
seemed to me favourable enough—of course, there was a
little of the *de haut en bas* business—you know how young
fellows like to write—but it was favourable—very favourable, I should say—however, she chose to work up a pretty
high old row on the strength of it when she came home,
and I had my work cut out for me before I could pacify
her. Why, you don't say she's at that again? Women
are such curious creatures; they hold on to things so; I
wonder, now, why it is she takes such an interest in that
fellow—after all this time?'

'Just as likely as not the merest coincidence—some
trifle that got hold of her brain when she first became
delirious,' the young Doctor said. 'I suppose the boating,
and the lake, and all that, brought back recollections of the
Highlands; and she seems to have been fascinated by the
life over there—the wildness of it caught her imagination,
I suppose. She must have been in considerable danger

once or twice, I should guess ; or perhaps she is mixing that up with the mishap of the other day. Well, I know I wish her father were here. We can't do more than what is being done; still, I wish he were here. If he can get through to Glen Falls to-night, you may depend on it he'll come along somehow.'

By this time Jack Huysen was nervously pacing up and down—there was no one but themselves in the room.

'Now, look here, Tom,' he said, presently, 'I wish you would tell me, honour bright : was it a squall that caught the boat, or was it downright carelessness on my part? I may as well know. I can't take more shame to myself anyhow—and to let you jump in after her, too, when I'm a better swimmer than you are—I must have lost my head altogether——'

'And much good you'd have done if you had jumped in,' the Doctor said, 'and left the two women to manage the boat. How should we have got picked up, then?'

'But about that gybing, now—was it my fault?'

'No, it was mine,' the Doctor said curtly. 'I shouldn't have given up the tiller. Fact is, the girls were just mad about that "Dancing in the Barn"; and I was fool enough to yield to them. I tell you, Jack, it isn't half as easy as it looks steering a boat that's running fair before the wind; I don't blame you at all ; I dare say there was a nasty puff that caught you when you weren't looking; anyhow, it's a blessing no one was hit by the boom—that was what I feared at first for Miss Hodson when I found her insensible—I was afraid she had been hit about the head——'

'And you don't think it was absolute carelessness?' the

other said quickly. 'Mind, I was steering straight for the pier, as you said.'

'Oh, well,' said the young Doctor evasively, 'if you had noticed in time, you know—or when I called to you—but perhaps it was too late then. It's no use going back on that now; what we have to do now is to fight this fever as well as we can.'

'I would take it over from her if I could,' Jack Huysen said, 'and willingly enough.'

It was not until early the next morning that Mr. Hodson arrived. He looked dreadfully pale and harassed and fatigued; for the fact was he was not in Chicago when they telegraphed for him; some business affairs had called him away to the south; and the news of his daughter's illness followed him from place to place until it found him in a remote corner of Louisiana, whence he had travelled night and day without giving himself an hour's rest. And now he would not stay to dip his hands and face in cold water after his long and anxious journey; he merely asked a few hurried questions of the Doctor; and then, stealthily and on tip-toe, and determined to show no sign of alarm or perturbation, he went into Carry's room.

She had been very delirious during the night—talking wildly and frantically in spite of all their efforts to soothe her; but now she lay exhausted, with the flushed face, and bluish lips, and eager, restless eyes so strangely unlike the Carry of other days. She recognised him at once—but not as a new-comer; she appeared to think he had been there all the time.

'Have you seen him, pappa?' she said, in that eager way. 'Did you see him when you were out?'

'Who, darling?' he said, as he sate down beside her and took her wasted hand in his.

'Why, Ronald, to be sure! Oh, something dreadful was about to happen to him—I don't know what it was—something dreadful and dreadful—and I called out—at the window—at the window there—and nurse says it is all right now—all right now——'

'Oh yes, indeed,' her father said gently, 'you may depend it is all right with Ronald now. Don't you fret about that.'

'Ah, but we neglected him, pappa, we neglected him; and I worst of any,' she went on, in that panting, breathless way. 'It was always the same—always thinking of doing something for him, and never doing it. I meant to have written to the innkeeper for his address in Glasgow; but no—that was forgotten too. And then the spliced rod, that George was to have got for me—I wanted Ronald to have the best salmon-rod that America could make—but it was all talking—all talking. Ah, it was never talking with him when he could do us a service—and the other boatmen getting money, of course—and he scarcely a "thank you" when we came away. Why didn't George get the fishing-rod?——'

'It's all right, Carry, darling,' her father said, whispering to her, 'you lie quiet now, and get well, and you'll see what a splendid salmon-rod we'll get for Ronald. Not that it would be of much use to him, you see, when he's in Glasgow with his books and studies; but it will show him we have not forgotten him. Don't you trouble about it, now; I will see it is all right; and you will give it to him yourself, if we go over there next spring, to try the salmon-fishing again.'

'Then you will take George with you, pappa,' she said, regarding him with her burning eyes.

' Oh yes ; and you——'

'Not me, not me,' she said, shaking her head.   'I am going away.   The Doctor doesn't know ; I know.   They have been very kind ; but—but—ask them, pappa, not to bother me to take things now—I want to be let alone, now you are here—it will only be for a little while——'

' Why, what nonsense you talk ! ' he said—but his heart was struck with a sudden fear, for these few straggling sentences she had uttered without any appearance of delirium. ' I tell you, you must hasten to get well and strong ; for when George and you and I go to Scotland, there will be a great deal of travelling to do.   You know we've got to fix on that piece of land, and see how it is all to be arranged and managed, so that George will have a comfortable little estate of his own when he comes of age ; or maybe, if it is a pretty place, we may be selfish and keep it in our own hands—eh, Carry ?—and then, you see, we shall have to have Ronald travel about with us, to give us his advice ; and the weather may be bad, you know, you'll have to brace yourself up. There, now, I'm not going to talk to you any more just now.   Lie still and quiet ; and mind you do everything the Doctor bids you—why, you to talk like that !—you ! I never thought you would give in, Carry : why, even as a schoolgirl you had the pluck of a dozen !   Don't you give in ; and you'll see if we haven't those two cobles out on Loch Naver before many months are over.'

She shook her head languidly ; her eyes were closed now.   And he was for slipping out of the room but that she clung to his hand for a moment.

' Pappa,' she said, in a low voice, and she opened her

eyes and regarded him—and surely at this moment, as he said to himself, she seemed perfectly sane and reasonable, ' I want you to promise me something.'

' Yes, yes,' he said quickly : what was it he would not have promised in order to soothe and quiet her mind at such a time ?

' I don't know about going with you and George,' she said, slowly, and apparently with much difficulty. ' It seems a long way off—a long time—and—and I hardly care now what happens. But you will look after Ronald ; you must promise me that, pappa ; and tell him I was sorry ; I suppose he heard the shooting was taken, and would know why we did not go over in the autumn ; but you will find him out, pappa, and see what he is doing ; and don't let him think we forgot him altogether.'

' Carry, darling, you leave that to me ; it will be all right with Ronald, I promise you,' her father said eagerly. ' Why, to think you should have been worrying about that ! Oh ! you will see it will be all right about Ronald, never fear !— what would you say, now, if I were to telegraph to him to come over and see you, if only you make haste and get well ?'

These assurances, at all events, seemed to pacify her somewhat ; and as she now lay still and quiet, her father stole out of the room, hoping that perhaps the long-prayed-for sleep might come to calm the fevered brain.

But the slow hours passed, and, so far from any improvement becoming visible, her condition grew more and more serious. The two doctors—for Doctor Tilley had summoned in additional aid—were assiduous enough ; but, when questioned, they gave evasive answers ; and when Mr. Hodson begged to be allowed to telegraph to a celebrated

Boston physician, who was also a particular friend of his own, asking him to come along at once, they acquiesced, it is true, but it was clearly with the view of satisfying Mr. Hodson's mind, rather than with any hope of advantage to the patient. From him, indeed, they scarcely tried to conceal the extreme gravity of the case. Emma Kerfoot and Mrs. Lalor were quieted with vague assurances ; but Mr. Hodson knew of the peril in which his daughter lay ; and, as it was impossible for him to go to sleep, and as his terrible anxiety put talking to these friends out of the question, he kept mostly to his own room, walking up and down, and fearing every moment lest direr news should arrive. For they had been much of companions, these two ; and she was an only daughter ; and her bright, frank, lovable character— that he had watched from childhood growing more and more beautiful and coming into closer communion with himself as year after year went by—had wound its tendrils round his heart. That Carry, of all people in the world, should be taken away from them so, seemed so strange and unaccountable : she that was ever so full of life and gaiety and confidence. The mother had been an invalid during most of her married life ; the boy George had not the strongest of constitutions ; but Carry was always to the fore with her audacious spirits and light-heartedness, ready for anything, and the best of travelling companions. And if she were to go, what would his life be to him ?—the light of it gone, the gladness of it vanished for ever.

That afternoon the delirium returned ; and she became more and more wildly excited ; until the paroxysm passed beyond all bounds. She imagined that Ronald was in some deadly peril ; he was alone, with no one to help ; his enemies had hold of him ; they were carrying him off, to thrust him into some black lake; she could hear the waters roaring in the dark.   It was in vain that the nurse tried to calm her and to reason with her; the wild, frightened eyes were fixed on vacancy; and again and again she made as if she would rush to his help, and would then sink back exhausted and moaning, and heaping reproaches on those who were allowing Ronald to be stricken down unaided. Then the climax came, quite unexpectedly.   The nurse—who happened at the moment to be alone with her in the room—went to the side-table for some more ice; and she was talking as she went; and trying to make her charge believe that everything was going on well enough with this friend of hers in Scotland.   But all of a sudden, when the nurse's back was thus turned, the girl sprang from the bed and rushed to the window.   She tore aside the curtains that had been tied together to deaden the light; she tugged and strained at the under sash; she was for throwing herself out—to fly to Ronald's succour.

'See, see, see!' she cried, and she wrenched herself away from the nurse's frightened grasp.   'Oh, don't you see that they are killing him—they are killing him—and none to help!   Ronald—Ronald!   Oh, what shall I do? Nurse, nurse, help me with the window—quick—quick— oh, don't you hear him calling?—and they are driving him down to the lake—he will be in the water soon—and lost —lost—lost—Ronald!—Ronald!—'

Nay, by this time she had actually succeeded in raising the under sash of the window a few inches—notwithstanding that the nurse clung round her, and tried to hold her arms, while she uttered shriek after shriek to call attention; and there is no doubt that the girl, grown quite frantic, would have succeeded in opening the window and throwing herself out, had not Mrs. Lalor, alarmed by the shrieking of the nurse, rushed in. Between them they got her back into bed; and eventually she calmed down somewhat; for, indeed, this paroxysm had robbed her of all her remaining strength. She lay in a kind of stupor now; she paid no heed to anything that was said to her; only her eyes were restless—when any one entered the room.

Dr. Tilley was with her father; the younger man was apparently calm, though rather pale; Mr. Hodson made no effort to conceal his agony of anxiety.

'I can only tell you what is our opinion,' the young Doctor said, speaking for himself and his brother practitioner. 'We should be as pleased as you could be to have Dr. Macartney here; but the delay—well, the delay might prove dangerous. Her temperature is 107—you know what that means?'

'But this rolling up in a wet sheet—there is a risk, isn't there?' the elder man said; and how keenly he was watching the expression of the young Doctor's face!

'I have only seen it used in extreme cases,' was the answer. 'If she were my own daughter, or sister, that is what I would do.'

'You have a right to speak—you have already saved her life once,' her father said.

'If we could only bring about a profuse perspiration,' the young Doctor said, a little more eagerly—for he had been maintaining a professionally dispassionate manner; 'and then if that should end in a long deep sleep—everything would go well then. But at present every hour that passes is against us—and her temperature showing no sign of abating.'

'Very well,' her father said, after a moment's involuntary

hesitation. 'If you say the decision rests with me, I will decide. We will not wait for Macartney. Do what you propose to do—I know you think it is for the best.'

And so it proved. Not once, but twice, within a space of seven days, had this young Doctor saved Carry Hodson's life. That evening they were all seated at dinner in the big dining-hall—Mrs. Lalor and her sister, Jack Huysen, and Carry's father—though the food before them did not seem to concern them much. They were talking amongst themselves, but rather absently and disconnectedly; and, what was strange enough, they spoke in rather low tones, as if that were of any avail. Dr. Tilley came in, and walked quickly up to the table; and quite unwittingly he put his hand on Emma Kerfoot's shoulder.

'I have good news,' said he, and there was a kind of subdued triumph in his eyes. 'She is sleeping as soundly—as soundly as any human being ever slept—everything has come off well—why, I am as happy as if I had been declared President!' But instantly he perceived that this exuberance of triumph was not in accordance with professional gravity. 'I think there is every reason to be satisfied with the prospect,' he continued in more measured tones, 'and now that Dr. Sargent is with her, and the night nurse just come down, I think I will take the opportunity to get something to eat—for I have forgotten about that since breakfast.'

'Oh, Tom, !' cried Miss Kerfoot reproachfully; and presently everybody at the table was showering attentions on this young man.

'And may I go in and see her now?' said Miss Kerfoot, preparing to steal away.

'No,' was the peremptory answer. 'No one. Every half hour of a sleep like that is worth its weight in gold—

well, that's a muddle, but you know what I mean. It's worth a cart-load of gold, anyway. I hope she'll go on for twenty-four hours, or thirty-six, for the matter of that. Oh, I can tell you it is quite refreshing to look at her—talk about the sleep of an infant!—you never saw an infant sleeping as deep and sound as that; and I shouldn't wonder now if her temperature were down another degree by midnight.'

But he saw that Mr. Hodson was still terribly agitated.

' Well, sir, would you like to go in and see her for a moment ? I have told the nurse to leave the door half an inch open, and there's a screen to keep off the draught ; I dare say we can slip in without disturbing her.'

And so it was that Mr. Hodson saw his daughter again —not with flushed cheeks and dilated eye, but lying still and calm, a very weight of sleep appearing to rest on her eyelids. And when he came out of the room again, he pressed the young man's hand—it was a message of thanks too deep for words.

All that night she slept ; and all next day she slept, without a moment's intermission. When, at length, she opened her eyes, and stirred a little, Emma Kerfoot was by the bedside in an instant.

' Dear Carry !' she said. ' Do you want anything ? '

She shook her head slightly; she was excessively weak ; but the look in her eyes was one of calm intelligence ; it was clear that the delirium had left her.

' Do you know that your father is here ? '

' Why ? ' she managed to say.

' Because you have been so ill ! Don't you know ? Don't you recollect ? '

'Yes—I know, a little,' she said. 'Where is Jack Huysen?'

'He is here in the hotel too. Oh, how glad they will all be to hear that you are quite yourself again. And I must go and tell them, as soon as nurse comes; for, you know, you'll have a long pull before you, Carry; and if you don't get quite well again not one of us will ever forgive ourselves for bringing you to Lake George. And there's Jack Huysen, poor fellow, he has just been distracted; and all the time you were ill you never had a word for him—though he used to haunt the passage outside just like a ghost—well, well, you'll have to make it up to him.'

At this moment the nurse appeared, and Miss Kerfoot was free to depart on her joyful errand. Of course, she was for summoning everybody—and Jack Huysen among the rest; but the doctors interposed; their patient must be kept perfectly quiet; in the meantime no one but her father was to have access to her room.

Now Mr. Hodson, when he was seated there by her side, and chatting lightly and carelessly about a variety of indifferent matters (she herself being forbidden to speak), considered that he could not do better than relieve her mind of any anxiety she may have entertained on Ronald's account. All through her delirium that was the one thing that seemed to trouble her; and, lest she should revert to it, he thought he might as well give her ample assurance that Ronald should be looked after. However, to his great surprise, he found that she was quite ignorant of her having made these appeals on behalf of Ronald. She did not seem to know that she had been in dire distress about him, reproaching herself for their treatment of him, and

begging her father to make such atonement as was yet possible. No ; when she was allowed to speak a little, she
said quite calmly that it was a pity they had not been able
to go to Scotland that autumn ; that they should have
written to Ronald to see how he was getting on ; and that
her father, if he visited the old country, in the coming
spring, ought surely to seek him out, and remind him that
he had some friends in America who would be glad to hear
of his welfare. But Mr. Hodson said to himself that
he would do a little more than that. He was not going
to recall the promise that he had made to his daughter
when, as he thought, she lay near to the very gates of death.
What had put that pathetic solicitude into her mind he
knew not ; but she had made her appeal, with dumb fever-
stricken eyes and trembling voice ; and he had answered
her and pledged his word. Ronald should be none the
loser that this sick girl had thought of him when that she
seemed to be vanishing away from them for ever ; surely
in that direction, as well as any other, the father might fitly
give his thank-offering—for the restitution to life of the
sole daughter of his house ?

CHAPTER XIII

LOCH NAVER lay calm and still under the slow awakening of the dawn. All along the eastern horizon the low-lying hills were of a velvet-textured olive-green—a mysterious shadow-land where no detail was visible; but overhead the skies were turning to a clear and luminous gray; the roseate tinge was leaving the upper slopes of Ben Loyal and Ben Clebrig; and the glassy surface of the lake was gradually whitening as the red-golden light changed to silver and broadened up and through the wide sleeping world. An intense silence lay over the little hamlet among the trees; not even a dog was stirring; but a tiny column of pale blue smoke issuing from one of the chimneys told that some one was awake within—probably the yellow-haired Nelly, whose duties began at an early hour.

And what was Meenie—or Rose Meenie, or Love Meenie, as she might be called now, after having all those things written about her—what was she doing awake and up at such a time? At all events, her morning greeting was there confronting her. She had brought it and put it on the little dressing-table; and as she brushed out her beautiful abundant brown tresses, her eyes went back again and again to the pencilled lines, and she seemed not ill-pleased. For this was what she read :

The hinds are feeding upon the hill,
And the hares on the fallow lea ;
    Awake, awake, Love Meenie !
Birds are singing in every tree ;

And roses you'll find on your window-sill
To scent the morning air ;
    Awake, awake, Love Meenie,
For the world is shining fair !

O who is the mistress of bird and flower ?
Ben Clebrig knows, I ween !
    Awake, awake, Love Meenie,
To show them their mistress and queen !

And it could hardly be expected that she should bring any very keen critical scrutiny to bear on these careless verses of Ronald's (of which she had now obtained a goodly number, by dint of wheedling and entreaty, and even downright insistence), seeing that nearly all of them were written in her praise and honour; but even apart from that she had convinced herself that they were very fine indeed; and that one or two of them were really pathetic; and she was not without the hope that, when the serious affairs of life had been attended to, and a little leisure and contemplation become possible, Ronald might turn to his poetical labours again and win some little bit of a name for himself amongst a few sympathetic souls here and there. That he could do so, if he chose, she was sure enough. It was all very well for him to make light of these scraps and fragments ; and to threaten to destroy them if she revealed the fact of their existence to anybody; but she knew their worth, if he did not ; and when, in this or that magazine or review, she saw a piece of poetry mentioned with praise, her first impulse was to quickly read it in order to ask herself whether Ronald—given time and opportunity—could

not have done as well. Moreover, the answer to that
question was invariably the same; and it did not leave her
unhappy. It is true (for she would be entirely dispassionate) he had not written anything quite so fine as 'Christabel'
—as yet; but the years were before him; she had confidence; the world should see—and give him a fitting welcome all in good time.

When, on this clear morning, she was fully equipped
for her walk, she stole silently down the stair, and made
her way out into the now awakening day. The little
hamlet was showing signs of life. A stable-lad was trying
to get hold of a horse that had strayed into the meadow;
a collie was barking its excitement over this performance;
the pretty Nelly appeared carrying an armful of clothes to
be hung out to dry. And then, as Meenie passed the inn,
she was joined by Harry the terrier, who, after the first
grovelling demonstrations of joy, seemed to take it for
granted that he was to be allowed to accompany her. And
she was nothing loth. The fact was, she was setting out
in quest of that distant eyrie of Ronald's of which he had
often told her; and she doubted very much whether she
would be able to find it; and she considered that perhaps
the little terrier might help her. Would he not naturally
make for his master's accustomed resting-place, when they
were sufficiently high up on the far Clebrig slopes?

So they went away along the road together; and she
was talking to her companion; and telling him a good deal
more about Glasgow, and about his master, than probably he
could understand. Considering, indeed, that this young
lady had just been sent home in deep disgrace, she seemed
in excellent spirits. She had borne the parting admonitions
and upbraidings of her sister Agatha with a most astonish-

ing indifference; she had received her mother's reproaches with a placid equanimity that the little woman could not understand at all (only that Meenie's face once or twice grew fixed and proud when there was some scornful reference to Ronald); and she had forthwith set about nursing her father—who had caught a severe chill and was in bed —with an amiable assiduity, just as if nothing had happened. As regards her father, he either did not know, or had refused to know, about Meenie's lamentable conduct. On this one point he was hopelessly perverse; he never would listen to anything said against this daughter of his; Meenie was always in the right—no matter what it was. And so, notwithstanding that she had been sent home as one in disgrace, and had been received as one in disgrace, she installed herself as her father's nurse with an amazing self-content; and she brought him his beef-tea and port-wine at the stated intervals (for the good Doctor did not seem to have as much faith in drugs as might have been anticipated); and she kept the peat-fire piled up and blazing; and she methodically read to him the *Inverness Courier*, the *Glasgow Weekly Citizen*, and the *Edinburgh Scotsman*; and when these were done she would get out a volume of old ballads, or perhaps 'The Eve of St. Agnes,' or 'Esmond,' or 'As You Like It,' or the 'Winter's Tale.' It did not matter much to him what she read; he liked to hear the sound of Meenie's voice—in this hushed, half-slumberous, warm little room, while the chill north winds howled without, chasing each other across the driven loch, and sighing and sobbing away along the lonely Strath-Terry.

But on this fair morning there was not a breath stirring; and the curving bays and promontories and birch-woods, and the far hills beyond, were all reflected in the magic

mirror of the lake, as she sped along the highway, making
for the Clebrig slopes. And soon she was mounting these
—with the light step of one trained to the heather; and
ever as she got higher and higher the vast panorama around
her grew wider and more wide, until she could see hills
and lochs and wooded islands that never were visible from
Inver-Mudal. In the perfect silence, the sudden whirr of
a startled grouse made her heart jump. A hare—that
looked remarkably like a cat, for there was as much white
as bluish-brown about it—got up almost at her feet and
sped swiftly away over heath and rock until it disappeared
in one of the numerous peat-hags. There was a solitary
eagle slowly circling in the blue; but at so great a height
that it was but a speck. At one moment she thought she
had caught sight of the antlers of a stag; and for a second
she stopped short, rather frightened; but presently she had
convinced herself that these were but two bits of withered
birch, appearing over the edge of a rock far above her. It
was a little chillier here; but the brisk exercise kept her
warm. And still she toiled on and on; until she knew, or
guessed, that she was high enough; and now the question
was to discover the whereabouts of the clump of rocks under
shelter of which Ronald was accustomed to sit, when he
had been up here alone, dreaming day-dreams, and scribbling
the foolish rhymes that had won to her favour, whatever he
might think of them.

At first this seemed a hopeless task; for the whole place
was a wilderness of moss and heather and peat-hags, with
scarcely a distinctive feature anywhere. But she wandered
about, watching the little terrier covertly; and at last she
saw him put his nose in an inquiring way into a hole underneath some tumbled boulders. He turned and looked at

her ; she followed. And now there could be no doubt that
this was Ronald's halting-place and pulpit of meditation ;
for she forthwith discovered the hidden case at the back of
the little cave—though the key of that now belonged to his
successor. And so, in much content, she sate herself down
on the heather ; with all the wide, sunlit, still world mapped
out before her—the silver thread of Mudal Water visible
here and there among the moors, and Loch Meadie with
its islands, and Ben Hope and Ben Loyal, and Bonnie
Strath-Naver, and the far Kyle of Tongue close to the
northern Sea.

Now, what had Love Meenie climbed all this height for ?
what but to read herself back into the time when Ronald
used to come here alone ; and to think of what he had
been thinking ; and to picture herself as still an unconscious maiden wandering about that distant little hamlet
that seemed but two or three dots down there among the
trees. This, or something like it, has always been a
favourite pastime with lovers ; but Meenie had an additional
source of interest in the possession of a packet of those idle
rhymes, and these were a kind of key to bygone moods
and days. And so it was here—in this strange stillness—
that Ronald had written these verses about her ; and perhaps caught a glimpse of her, with his telescope, as she
came out from the cottage to intercept the mail ; when
little indeed was she dreaming that he had any such fancies
in his head. And now as she turned over page after page,
sometimes she laughed a little, when she came to something
that seemed a trifle audacious—and she scarcely wondered
that he had been afraid of her seeing such bold declara-
tions : and then again a kind of compunction filled her
heart ; and she wished that Ronald had not praised her

so ; for what had she done to deserve it ; and how would
her coming life be made to correspond with these all too
generous and exalted estimates of her character?   Of
course she liked well enough to come upon praises of her
abundant brown hair, and her Highland eyes, and the rose-
leaf tint of her cheeks, and the lightness of her step ; for
she was aware of these things as well as he ; and glad
enough that she possessed them, for had they not com-
mended her to him?   But as for these other wonderful
graces of mind and disposition with which he had adorned
her?   She was sadly afraid that he would find her stupid,
ill-instructed, unread, fractious, unreasonable, incapable of
understanding him.   Look, for example, how he could
imbue these hills and moors and vales with a kind of magic,
so that they seemed to become his personal friends.   To
her they were all dead things (except Mudal Water, at
times, on the summer evenings), but to him they seemed
instinct with life.   They spoke to him ; and he to them ;
he understood them; they were his companions and friends;
who but himself could tell of what this very hill of Clebrig
was thinking?—

Ben Clebrig's a blaze of splendour
In the first red flush of the morn,
And his gaze is fixed on the eastward
To greet the day new-born ;
And he listens a-still for the bellow
Of the antlered stag afar,
And he laughs at the royal challenge,
The hoarse, harsh challenge of war.

But Ben Clebrig is gentle and placid
When the sun sinks into the west,
And a mild and a mellow radiance
Shines on his giant crest ;

For he's looking down upon Meenie
As she wanders along the road,
And the mountain bestows his blessing
On the fairest child of God.

There again : what could he see in her (she asked herself)
that he should write of her so? He had declared to her
that the magic with which all this neighbourhood was
imbued was due to her presence there ; but how could she,
knowing herself as she did, believe that? And how to
show her gratitude to him ; and her faith in him ; and her
confidence as to the future? Well, she could but give to
him her life and the love that was the life of her life—if
these were worth the taking.

But there was one among these many pieces that she
had pondered over which she returned to again and again,
and with a kind of pride ; and that not because it sounded
her praises, but because it assured her hopes. As for
Ronald's material success in life, she was troubled with
little doubt about that. It might be a long time before he
could come to claim his wife; but she was content to wait;
in that direction she had no fears whatever. But there
was something beyond that. She looked forward to the
day when even the Stuarts of Glengask and Orosay should
know what manner of man this was whom she had chosen
for her husband. Her mother had called him an un-
educated peasant; but she paid no heed to the taunt;
rather she was thinking of the time when Ronald—other
things being settled—might perhaps go to Edinburgh, and
get to know some one holding the position there that
Jeffrey used to hold (her reading was a little old-fashioned)
who would introduce him to the world of letters and open
the way to fame. She knew nothing of Carry Hodson's

luckless attempt in this direction ; she knew, on the contrary, that Ronald was strongly averse from having any of these scraps printed ; but she said to herself that the fitting time would come. And if these unpolished verses are found to belie her confident and proud prognostications as to the future, let it be remembered that she was hardly nineteen, that she was exceedingly warm-hearted, that she was a young wife, and day and night with little to think about but the perfections of her lover, and his kindness to her, and his praise of her, and the honour in which he held her. However, this piece was not about Meenie at all—he had called it

BY ISLAY'S SHORES.

By Islay's shores she sate and sang :
*   ' O winds, come blowing o'er the sea,*
And bring me back my love again
*   That went to fight in Germanie !'*

And all the livelong day she sang,
*   And nursed the bairn upon her knee :*
' Balou, balou, my bonnie bairn,
*   Thy father's far in Germanie,*

But ere the summer days are gane,
*   And winter blackens bush and tree,*
Thy father will we welcome hame
*   Frae the red wars in Germanie.'*

O dark the night fell, dark and mirk ;
*   A wraith stood by her icily :*
' Dear wife, I'll never more win hame,
*   For I am slain in Germanie.*

On Minden's field I'm lying stark,
*   And Heaven is now my far countrie,*
Farewell, dear wife, farewell, farewell,
*   I'll ne'er win hame frae Germanie.'*

And all the year she came and went,
And wandered wild frae sea to sea ;
' *O neighbours, is he ne'er come back,*
My love that went to Germanie ? '

Port Ellen saw her many a time ;
Round by Port Askaig wandered she :
' *Where is the ship that's sailing in*
With my dear love frae Germanie ? '

But when the darkened winter fell :
' *It's cold for baith my bairn and me ;*
Let me lie down and rest awhile :
My love's away frae Germanie.

O far away and away he dwells ;
High Heaven is now his fair countrie ;
And there he stands—with arms outstretched—
To welcome hame my bairn and me ! '

And if Mcenie's eyes were filled with tears when she
had re-read the familiar lines, her heart was proud enough ;
and all her kinsmen of Glengask and Orosay had no terrors
for her ; and her mother's taunts no sting. Of course, all
this that she hoped for was far away in the future ; but
even as regarded the immediate years before her she refused
to be harassed by any doubt. Perhaps she would not have
asserted in set terms that a knack of stringing verses together
proved that the writer had also the capacity and knowledge
and judgment necessary to drain and fence and plant and
stock a Highland estate ; abstract questions of the kind had
little interest for her ; what she did know—what formed the
first article of her creed, and the last, and the intervening
thirty-seven—was that Ronald could do anything he put
his mind to. And this was a highly useful and comfortable
belief, considering all her circumstances.

And so she sped away down the mountain-side again—
glad to have discovered Ronald's retreat ; and so light and

swift was her step that when she at length reached the inn she found herself just ahead of the mail coming in from the south. Of course she waited for letters; and when Mrs. Murray had opened the bags, it was found there were three for the Doctor's cottage. The first was from Ronald; that Meenie whipped into her pocket. The second was for Mrs. Douglas, and clearly in Agatha's handwriting. The third, addressed to Meenie, had an American stamp on it; and this was the one that she opened and read as she quietly walked homeward.

It was a long letter; and it was from Miss Carry Hodson; who first of all described the accident that had befallen her, and her subsequent illness; and plainly intimated that no such thing would have happened had her Highland friends been in charge of the boat. Then she went on to say that her father had just sailed for Europe; that he had business to transact in Scotland; that he wished to see Ronald; and would Miss Douglas be so very kind as to ask the innkeeper, or the post-master at Lairg, or any one who knew Ronald's address in Glasgow, to drop a post-card to her father, addressed to the Langham Hotel, London, with the information. Moreover, her father had intimated his intention of taking the Loch Naver salmon-fishing for the next season, if it was not as yet let; and in that case the writer would be overjoyed to find herself once more among her Inver-Mudal friends. Finally, and as a kind of reminder and keepsake, she had sent by her father a carriage-rug made mostly of chipmunk skins; and she would ask Miss Douglas's acceptance of it; and hoped that it would keep her knees snug and warm and comfortable when the winds were blowing too sharply along Strath-Terry.

Of course, all this was wonderful news to come to such

a quiet and remote corner of the world; but there was other news as well; and that by an odd coincidence. Some little time after Mrs. Douglas had received the letter from Agatha, she came to Meenie.

'Williamina,' said she, 'Agatha writes to me about Mr. Frank Lauder.'

'Yes?' said Meenie, rather coldly.

'He intends renting the salmon-fishing on the loch for the next season; and he will be alone at the inn. Agatha hopes that we shall be particularly civil to him; and I hope —I say, I hope—that every one in this house will be. It is of the greatest importance, considering how he stands with regard to Mr. Gemmill. I hope he will be received in this house with every attention and kindness.'

And then the pompous little dame left. It was almost a challenge she had thrown down; and Meenie was at first a little bewildered. What then?—would this young man, for the six weeks or two months of his stay, be their constant visitor? He would sit in the little parlour, evening after evening; and how could she keep him from talking to her, and how could she keep him from looking at her? And Ronald—her husband—would be far away; and alone, perhaps; and not allowed a word with her; whereas she would have to be civil and polite to this young man; and even if she held her eyes downcast, how could she help his regarding her face?

And then she suddenly bethought her of Miss Hodson's letter. What?—was Mr. Hodson after the fishing too? And ought not the last tenant to have the refusal? And should not the Duke's agent know? And why should she not write him a note—just in case no inquiry had been made? She had not much time to think about the matter;

but she guessed quickly enough that, if an American millionaire and the son of a Glasgow merchant are after the same thing, and that thing purchasable, the American is likely to get it. And why should Ronald's wife be stared at and talked to by this young man—however harmless and amiable his intentions?

So she went swiftly to her own room and wrote as follows :—

'DEAR MR. CRAWFORD—I have just heard from Miss Hodson, whose father was here last spring, that he is on his way to Europe; and that he hopes to have the fishing again this year. I think I ought to let you know, just in case you should have any other application for the loch. I am sure Miss Hodson will be much disappointed if he does not get it. Yours sincerely,

'MEENIE S. DOUGLAS.'

''There,' said she, and there was a little smile of triumph about her mouth, 'if that doesn't put a spoke in the wheel of Mr. Frank Lauder, poor fellow, I don't know what will.'

'Spiteful little cat,' her sister Agatha would have called her, had she known; but women's judgments of women are not as men's.

CHAPTER XIV

WANDERINGS IN THE WEST.

ON a singularly clear and brilliant morning in February a large and heavy screw-steamer slowly crept out of the land-locked little harbour of Portree, and steadily made away for the north. For her the squally Ben Inivaig at the mouth of the channel had no terrors; indeed, what could any vessel fear on such a morning as this? When they got well out into Raasay Sound, it seemed as if the whole world had been changed into a pantomime-scene. The sky was calm and cloudless; the sea was as glass and of the most dazzling blue; and those masses of white that appeared on that perfect mirror were the reflections of the snow-powdered islands—Raasay, and Fladda, and South Rona—that gleamed and shone and sparkled there in the sun. Not often are the wide waters of the Minch so fair and calm in mid-winter; the more usual thing is northerly gales, with black seas thundering by into Loch Staffin and Kil-maluag Bay, or breaking into sheets and spouts of foam along the headlands of Aird Point and Ru Hunish. This was as a holiday trip, but for the sharp cold. The islands were white as a solan's wing — save along the shores; the sea was of a sapphire blue; and when they got up by Rona light behold the distant snow-crowned hills of Ross and Cromarty rose faint and spectral and wonderful into the pale and summer-like sky.   The men sung '*Fhir a Bhata*' as they scoured the brass and scrubbed the decks ; the passengers marched up and down, clapping their hands to keep them warm ; and ever as the heavy steamer forged on its way, the world of blue sea and sky and snow-white hills opened out before them, until some declared at last that in the far north they could make out the Shiant Isles.

Now under shelter of the companion-way leading down into the saloon three men were standing, and two of them were engaged in an animated conversation.   The third, who was Mr. Hodson, merely looked on and listened, a little amused, apparently.   One of the others—a tall, heavy-bearded, north-Highland-looking man—was Mr. Carmichael, a famous estate-agent in London, who had run two or three commissions together as an excuse for this midwinter trip. The third member of the group was Ronald, who was hammering away in his usual dogmatic fashion.

'Pedigree?   The pride of having ancestors?' he was saying.   'Why, there's not a man alive whose ancestry does not stretch as far back as any other man's ancestry.   Take it any way ye like : if Adam was our grandfather, then we're all his grandchildren ; or if we are descended from a jellyfish or a monkey, the line is of the same length for all of us—for dukes, and kings, and herd-laddies.   The only difference is this, that some know the names of their fore-fathers, and some don't ; and the presumption is that the man whose people have left no story behind them is come of a more moral, useful, sober, hard-working race than the man whose forbears were famous cut-throats in the middle ages, or dishonest lawyers, or king's favourites.   It's plain John Smith that has made up the wealth of this country ;

and that has built her ships for her, and defended her, and put her where she is; and John Smith had his ancestors at Cressy and Agincourt as well as the rest—ay, and they had the bulk of the fighting to do, I'll be bound; but I think none the worse of him because he cannot tell you their names or plaster his walls with coats of arms. However, it's idle talking about a matter of sentiment, and that's the fact; and so, if you'll excuse me, I'll just go down into the cabin, and write a couple o' letters.'

A minute or so after he had disappeared, Mr. Hodson (who looked miserably cold, to tell the truth, though he was wrapped from head to heel in voluminous furs) motioned his companion to come a few yards aside, so that they could talk without fear of being overheard.

'Now,' said he, in his slow and distinct way, 'now we are alone, I want you to tell me what you think of that young man.'

'I don't like his politics,' was the prompt and blunt answer.

'No more do I,' said Mr. Hodson coolly. 'But for another reason. You call him a Radical, I call him a Tory. But no matter—I don't mean about politics. Politics?— who but a fool bothers his head about politics—unless he can make money out of them? No, I mean something more practical than that. Here have you and he been together these three days, talking about the one subject nearly all the time—I mean the management of these Highland estates, and the nature of the ground, and what should be done, and all that. Well, now, you are a man of great experience; and I want you to tell me what you think of this young fellow. I want you to tell me honestly; and it will be in strict confidence, I assure you. Now, has he got a good solid grip of the thing? Does he know? Does he catch on? Is he safe? Is he to be trusted?——'

'Oh, there, there, there!' said the big estate-agent, interrupting through mere. good-nature. ' 'That's quite another thing—quite another thing. I've not a word to say against him there—no, quite the other way—a shrewd-headed, capable fellow he is, with a groundwork of practical knowledge that no man ever yet got out of books. As sharp-eyed a fellow as I have come across for many a day —didn't you see how he guessed at the weak points of that Mull place before ever he set foot ashore? Quick at figures, too—oh yes, yes, a capable fellow I call him; he has been posting himself up, I can see; but it's where his practical knowledge comes in that he's of value. When it's a question of vineries, or something like that, then he goes by the book—that's useless.'

Mr. Hodson listened in silence; and his manner showed nothing.

'I have been thinking he would be a valuable man for me,' the agent said presently.

'In your office?' said Mr. Hodson, raising his eyes.

'Yes. And for this reason. You see, if he would only keep away from those d—d politics of his, he is a very good-natured fellow, and he has got an off-hand way with him that makes shepherds, and keepers, and people of that kind friendly; the result is that he gets all the information that he wants—and that isn't always an easy thing to get. Now if I had a man like that in my office, whom I could send with a client thinking of purchasing an estate—to advise him—to get at the truth—and to be an intelligent and agreeable travelling-companion at the same time—that would be a useful thing.'

'Say, now,' continued Mr. Hodson (who was attending mostly to his own meditations), 'do you think, from what you've seen of this young man, that he has the knowledge and business-capacity to be overseer—factor, you call it, don't you?—of an estate—not a large estate, but perhaps about the size of the one we saw yesterday or this one we are going to now? Would he go the right way about it? Would he understand what had to be done—I mean, in improving the land, and getting the most out of it——'

Mr. Carmichael laughed.

'It's not a fair question,' said he. 'Your friend Strang and I are too much of one opinion—ay, on every point we're agreed—for many's the long talk we've had over the matter.'

'I know—I know,' Mr. Hodson said. 'Though I was only half-listening; for when you got to feu-duties and public burdens and things of that kind I lost my reckoning. But you say that you and Strang are agreed as to the proper way of managing a Highland estate: very well: assuming your theories to be correct, is he capable of carrying them out?'

'I think so—I should say undoubtedly—I don't think I would myself hesitate about trusting him with such a place —that is, when I had made sufficient inquiries about his character, and got some money guarantee about his steward-ship. But then, you see, Mr. Hodson, I'm afraid, if you were to let Strang go his own way in working up an estate, so as to get the most marketable value into it, you and he would have different opinions at the outset. I mean with such an estate as you would find over there,' he added, indicating with his finger the long stretch of wild and mountainous country they were approaching. 'On rough and hilly land like that, in nine cases out of ten, you may depend on it, it's foresting that pays.'

'But that's settled,' Mr. Hodson retorted rather sharply. 'I have already told you, and Strang too, that if I buy a place up here I will not have a stag or a hind from end to end of it.'

'Faith, they're things easy to get rid of,' the other said good-naturedly. ''They'll not elbow you into the ditch if you meet them on the road.'

'No; I have heard too much. Why, you yourself said that the very name of American stank in the nostrils of the Highlanders.'

'Can you wonder?' said Mr. Carmichael quietly: they had been talking the night before of certain notorious doings, on the part of an American lessee, which were provoking much newspaper comment at the time.

'Well, what I say is this—if I buy a place in the High-lands—and no one can compel me to buy it—it is merely a fancy I have had for two or three years back, and I can give it up if I choose—but what I say is, if I do buy a place in the Highlands, I will hold it on such conditions that I shall be able to bring my family to live on it, and that I shall be able to leave it to my boy without shame. I will not associate myself with a system that has wrought such cruelty and tyranny. No; I will not allow a single acre to be forested.'

''There's such a quantity of the land good for nothing but deer,' Mr. Carmichael said, almost plaintively. 'If you only saw it!—you're going now by what the newspaper writers say—people who never were near a deer-forest in their lives.'

'Good for nothing but deer? But what about the black

cattle that Ronald—that Strang—is always talking about?'
was the retort—and Mr. Hodson showed a very unusual
vehemence, or, at least, impatience. 'Well, I don't care.
That has got nothing to do with me. But it has got to do
with my factor, or overseer, or whatever he is. And between him and me this is how it will lie: "If you can't
work my estate, big or small as it may be, without putting
the main part of it under deer, and beginning to filch
grazings here and there, and driving the crofters down to
the sea-shore, and preventing a harmless traveller from
having a Sunday walk over the hills, then out you go. You
may be fit for some other place: not for mine."' Then he
went on in a milder strain. 'And Strang knows that very
well. No doubt, if I were to put him in a position of trust
like that, he might be ambitious to give a good account of
his stewardship; I think, very likely he would be, for he's
a young man; but if I buy a place in the Highlands, it will
have to be managed as I wish it to be managed. When I
said that I wanted the most made out of the land, I did
not mean the most money. No. I should be glad to have
four per cent for my investment; if I can't have that, I
should be content with three; but it is not as a commercial
speculation that I shall go into the affair, if I go into it at
all. My wants are simple enough. As I tell you, I admire
the beautiful, wild country; I like the people—what little
I have seen of them; and if I can get a picturesque bit of
territory somewhere along this western coast, I should like
to give my family a kind of foothold in Europe, and I dare
say my boy might be glad to spend his autumns here, and
have a turn at the grouse. But for the most part of the
time the place would be under control of the factor; and
I want a factor who will work the estate under certain

specified conditions. First, no foresting. Then I would
have the crofts revalued—as fairly as might be; no crofter
to be liable to removal who paid his rent. The sheep-
farms would go by their market value, though I would not
willingly disturb any tenant; however, in that case, I should
be inclined to try Strang's plan of having those black cattle
on my own account. I would have the cottars taken away
from the crofts (allowing for the rent paid to the crofter,
for that would be but fair, when the value of the crofts was
settled), and I would build for them a model village, which
you might look upon as a philanthropic fad of my own, to
be paid for separately. No gratuitous grazing anywhere to
crofter or cottar; that is but the parent of subsequent
squabbles. Then I would have all the draining and plant-
ing and improving of the estate done by the local hands,
so far as that was practicable. And then I should want
four per cent return on the purchase-money; and I should
not be much disappointed with three; and perhaps (though
I would not admit this to anybody) if I saw the little com-
munity thriving and satisfied—and reckoning also the
honour and glory of my being a king on my own small
domain—I might even be content with two per cent. Now,
Mr. Carmichael, is this practicable? And is this young
fellow the man to undertake it? I would make it worth
his while. I should not like to say anything about payment
by results or percentage on profits; that might tempt him
to screw it out of the poorer people when he was left master
—though he does not talk like that kind of a fellow. I
wrote to Lord Ailine about him; and got the best of
characters. I went and saw the old man who is coaching
him for that forestry examination; he is quite confident
about the result—not that I care much about that my-

self. What do you say now? You ought to be able to judge.'

Mr. Carmichael hesitated.

'If you got the estate at a fair price,' he said at length, 'it might be practicable, though these improvement schemes suck in money as a sponge sucks in water. And as for this young fellow—well, I should think he would be just the man for the place—active, energetic, shrewd-headed, and a pretty good hand at managing folk, as I should guess. But, you know, before giving any one an important post like that—and especially with your going back to America for the best part of every year—I think you ought to have some sort of money guarantee as a kind of safeguard. It's usual. God forbid I should suggest anything against the lad—he's as honest looking as my own two boys, and I can say no more than that—still, business is business. A couple of sureties, now, of £500 apiece, might be sufficient.'

'It's usual?' repeated Mr. Hodson absently. 'Yes, I suppose it is. Pretty hard on a young fellow, though, if he can't find the sureties. A thousand pounds is a big figure for one in his position. He has told me about his father and his brother : they're not in it, anyhow—both of them with hardly a sixpence to spare. However, it's no use talking about it until we see whether this place here is satisfactory; and even then don't say a word about it to him ; for if some such post were to be offered to him— and if the securities were all right and so forth—it has got to be given to him as a little present from an American young lady, if you can call it a present when you merely propose to pay a man a fair day's wage for a fair day's work. And I am less hopeful now ; the three places we have looked at were clearly out of the question; and my Highland mansion may prove to be a castle in Spain after all.'

Late that night they reached their destination; and early next morning at the door of the hotel—which looked strangely deserted amid the wintry landscape—a waggonette was waiting for them, and also the agent for the estate they were going to inspect. They started almost directly; and a long and desperately cold drive it proved to be; Mr. Hodson, for one, was glad enough when they dismounted at the keeper's cottage where their tramp over the ground was to begin—he did not care how rough the country might be, so long as he could keep moving briskly.

Now it had been very clear during these past few days that Ronald had not the slightest suspicion that Mr. Hodson, in contemplating the purchase of a Highland estate (which was an old project of his), had also in his eye some scheme for Ronald's own advancement. All the way through he had been endeavouring to spy out the nakedness of the land, and to demonstrate its shortcomings. He considered that was his business. Mr. Hodson had engaged him— at what he considered the munificent terms of a guinea a day and all expenses paid—to come and give his advice; and he deemed it his duty to find out everything, especially whatever was detrimental, about such places as they visited, so that there should be no swindling bargain. And so on this Ross-shire estate of Balnavrain, he was proving himself a hard critic. This was hopelessly bleak; that was worth- less bog-land;—why was there no fencing along those cliffs?—where were the roads for the peats?—who had had control over the burning of the heather?—wasn't it strange that all along these tops they had not put up more than a couple of coveys of grouse, a hare or two, and a single ptarmigan ?   But all at once, when they had toiled across this unpromising and hilly wilderness, they came upon a scene of the most startling beauty—for now they were looking down and out on the western sea, that was a motionless mirror of blue and white ; and near them was a wall of picturesquely wooded cliffs ; and below that again, and sloping to the shore, a series of natural plateaus and carefully planted enclosures ; while stretching away inland was a fertile valley, with smart farmhouses, and snug clumps of trees, and a meandering river that had salmon ob- viously written on every square foot of its partially frozen surface.

'What a situation for a house !' was Ronald's involuntary exclamation—as he looked down on the sheltered semicircle below him, guarded on the east and north by the cliffs, and facing the shining west.

'I thought ye would say that,' the agent said, with a quiet smile.   'It's many's the time I've heard Sir James say he would give £20,000 if he could bring the Castle there ; and he was aye minded to build there—ay, even to the day of his death, poor man ; but then the Colonel, when the place came to him, said no ; he would rather sell Bal- navrain ; and maist likely the purchaser would be for build- ing a house to his ain mind.'

'And a most sensible notion too,' Mr. Hodson said. ' But look here, my friend : you've brought us up to a kind of Pisgah ; I would rather go down into that land of Gilead, and see what the farmhouses are like.'

'Ay, but I brought ye here because it's about the best place for giving ye an idea of the marches,' said the man imperturbably, for he knew his own business better than the stranger. ' Do ye see the burn away over there beyond the farmhouse?'

' Yes, yes.'

' Well, that's the Balnavrain march right up to the top; and then the Duchess runs all along the sky-line yonder— to the black scaur.'

'You don't say!' observed Mr. Hodson. 'I never heard of a Duchess doing anything so extraordinary.'

' But we march with the Duchess,' said the other, a little bewildered.

''That's a little more decorous, anyway. Well now, I suppose we can make all that out on the Ordnance Survey map when we get back to the hotel. I'm for getting down into the valley—to have a look around; I take it that if I lived here I shouldn't spend all the time on a mountain-top.'

Well, the long and the short of it was that, after having had two or three hours of laborious and diligent tramping and inspection and questioning and explanation, and after having been entertained with a comfortable meal of oat-cake and hot broth and boiled beef at a hospitable farmhouse, they set out again on their cold drive back to the hotel, where a long business conversation went on all the evening, during dinner and after dinner. It was very curious how each of these three brought this or that objection to the place—as if bound to do so; and how the fascination of the mere site of it had so clearly captivated them none the less. Of course, nothing conclusive was said or done that night; but, despite these deprecatory pleas, there was a kind of tacit and general admission that Balnavrain, with proper supervision and attention to the possibilities offered by its different altitudes, might be made into a very admirable little estate, with a dwelling-house on it second in point of situation to none on the whole western sea-board of the Highlands.

'Ronald,' said Mr. Hodson that evening, when Mr. Carmichael had gone off to bed (he was making for the south early in the morning), 'we have had some hard days' work; why should we let Loch Naver lie idle? I suppose we could drive from here somehow? Let us start off to-morrow; and we'll have a week's salmon-fishing.'

'To Inver-Mudal?' he said—and he turned quite pale.

'Yes, yes, why not?' Mr. Hodson answered. But he had noticed that strange look that had come across the younger man's face; and he attributed it to a wrong cause. 'Oh, it will not take up so much of your time,' he continued. 'Mr. Weems declares you must have your certificate as a matter of course. And as for expenses—the present arrangement must go on, naturally, until you get back to Glasgow. What is a week, man? Indeed, I will take no denial.'

And Ronald could not answer. To Inver-Mudal?—to meet the girl whom he dared not acknowledge to be his wife?—and with his future as hopelessly uncertain as ever. Once or twice he was almost driven to make a confession to this stranger, who seemed so frankly interested in him and his affairs; but no; he could not do that; and he went to bed wondering with what strange look in her eyes Meenie would find him in Inver-Mudal—if he found it impossible to resist the temptation of being once more within sight of her, and within hearing of the sound of her voice.

CHAPTER XV

MR. HODSON could by no means get to understand the half-expressed reluctance, the trepidation almost, with which Ronald seemed to regard this visit to Inver-Mudal. It was not a matter of time; for his studies for the examination were practically over. It was not a matter of expense; for he was being paid a guinea a day. It was not debt; on that point Mr. Hodson had satisfied himself by a few plain questions; and he knew to a sovereign what sum Ronald had still in the bank. Nor could he believe, after the quite unusual terms in which Lord Ailine had written about the young man's conduct and character, that Ronald was likely to have done anything to cause him to fear a meeting with his former friends. And so, having some little experience of the world, he guessed that there was probably a girl in the case; and discreetly held his peace.

But little indeed was he prepared for the revelation that was soon to be made. On the afternoon of one of these cold February days they were driving northward along Strath-Terry. A sprinkling of snow had fallen in the morning; the horses' hoofs and the wheels of the waggon-ette made scarcely any sound in this prevailing silence. They had come in sight of Loch Naver; and the long

sheet of water looked quite black amid the white undula-
tions of the woods and the moorland and the low-lying hills.
Now at this point the road leading down to the village
makes a sudden turn; and they were just cutting round
the corner when Ronald, who had been anxiously looking
forward, caught sight of that that most he longed and that
most he feared to see. It was Meenie herself—she was
walking by the side of the way, carrying some little parcel
in her hand; and they had come upon her quite unexpectedly, and noiselessly besides; and what might she not
betray in this moment of sudden alarm? He gripped the
driver's arm, thinking he might stop the horses; but it was
now too late for that. They were close to her; she heard
the patter of horses' hoofs; she looked up, startled; and
the next moment—when she saw Ronald there—she had
uttered a quick, sharp cry, and had staggered back a step
or so, until in her fright she caught at the wire fence behind
her. She did not fall; but her face was as white as the
snow around her; and when he leapt from the waggonette,
and seized her by both wrists, so as to hold her there, she
could only say, 'Ronald, Ronald,' and could seek for no
explanation of this strange arrival. But he held her tight
and firm; and with a wave of his hand he bade the driver
drive on and leave them. And Mr. Hodson lowered his
eyes, thinking that he had seen enough; but he formally
raised his hat, all the same; and as he was being driven
on to the inn, he returned to his surmise that there was a
girl in the case—only who could have imagined that it was
the Doctor's daughter?

Nor was there a single word said about this tell-tale
meeting when Ronald came along to the inn, some few
minutes thereafter. He seemed a little preoccupied, that

was all.   He rather avoided the stormy welcome that
greeted him everywhere; and appeared to be wholly bent
on getting the preparations pushed forward for the fishing
of the next day.   Of course everything had to be arranged;
for they had had no thought of coming to Inver-Mudal
when they sailed from Glasgow; there was not even a boat
on the loch, nor a single gillie engaged.

But later on that evening, when the short winter day
had departed, and the blackness of night lay over the land,
Ronald stole away from the inn, and went stealthily down
through the fields till he found himself by the side of the
river.   Of course, there was nothing visible; had he not
known every foot of the ground, he dared not have come
this way; but onward he went like a ghost through the
dark until he finally gained the bridge, and there he paused
and listened.   'Meenie!' he said, in a kind of whisper;
but there was no reply.   And so he groped his way to the
stone dyke by the side of the road, and sate down there,
and waited.

This was not how he had looked forward to meeting
Meenie again.   Many a time he had pictured that to himself—his getting back to Inver-Mudal after the long separa-
tion—the secret summons—and Meenie coming silently
out from the little cottage to join him.   But always the
night was a moonlight night; and the wide heavens calm
and clear; and Loch Naver rippling in silver under the
dusky shadows of Ben Clebrig.   Why, he had already
written out that summons; and he had sent it to Meenie;
and no doubt she had read it over to herself more than
once; and wondered when the happy time was to be.   The
night that he had looked forward to was more like a night
for a lovers' meeting: this was the message he had sent her—

O white's the moon upon the loch,
And black the bushes on the brae,
And red the light in your window-pane :
When will ye come away,
Meenie,
When will ye come away ?

I'll wrap ye round and keep ye warm,
For mony a secret we've to tell,
And ne'er a sound will hinder us
Down in yon hidden dell,
Meenie,
Down in yon hidden dell.

O see the moon is sailing on
Through fleecy clouds across the skies,
But fairer far the light that I know,
The love-light in your eyes,
Meenie,
The love-light in your eyes.

O haste and haste ; the night is sweet,
But sweeter far what I would hear ;
And I have a secret to tell to you,
A whisper in your ear,
Meenie,
A whisper in your ear.

But here was a bitter cold winter night ; and Meenie would have to come through the snow ; and dark as pitch it was—he would have to guess at the love-light in her eyes, so cruelly dense was this blackness all around.

Then his quick ear detected a faint sound in the distance — a hushed footfall on the snow; and that came nearer and nearer ; he went out to the middle of the road.

' Is that you, Meenie ? '

The answer was a whisper—

' Ronald ! '

And like a ghost she came to him through the dark;
but indeed this was no ghost at all that he caught to him
and that clung to him, for if her cheeks were cold her
breath was warm about his face, and her lips were warm,
and her ungloved hands that were round his neck were
warm, and all the furry wrappings that she wore could not
quite conceal the joyful beating of her heart.

'Oh, Ronald—Ronald—you nearly killed me with the
fright—I thought something dreadful had happened—that
you had come back without any warning—and now you
say instead that it's good news—oh, let it be good news,
Ronald—let it be good news—if you only knew how I
have been thinking and thinking—and crying sometimes—
through the long days and the long nights—let it be good
news that you have brought with you, Ronald!'

'Well, lass' (but this was said after some little time;
for he had other things to say to her with which we have
no concern here), 'it may be good news; but it's pretty
much guess-work; and maybe I'm building up something on my own conceit, that will have a sudden fall,
and serve me right. And then even at the best I hardly
see——'

'But, Ronald, you said it was good news!' And then
she altered her tone. 'Ah, but I don't care! I don't care
at all when you are here. It is only when you are away
that my heart is like lead all the long day; and at night I
lie and think that everything is against us—and such a long
time to wait—and perhaps my people finding out—but
what is it, Ronald, you had to tell me?'

'Well, now, Meenie,' said he.

'But that is not my name—to you,' said she; for indeed
she scarce knew what she said, and was all trembling, and

excited, and clinging to him—there, in the dark, mid the
wild waste of the snow.

'Love-Meenie and Rose-Meenie, all in one,' said he,
'listen, and I'll tell you now what maybe lies before us.
Maybe, it is, and that only; I think this unexpected coming
to see you may have put me off my head a bit; but if it's
all a mistake—well, we are no worse off than we were
before.   And this is what it is now : do you remember my
telling you that Mr. Hodson had often been talking of buy-
ing an estate in the Highlands?—well, he has just been
looking at one—it's over there on the Ross-shire coast—
and it's that has brought us to the Highlands just now, for
he would have me come and look at it along with him.
And what would you think if he made me the factor of it?
Well, maybe I'm daft to think of such a thing; but he has
been talking and talking in a way I cannot understand
unless some plan of that kind is in his head; ay, and he
has been making inquiries about me, as I hear; and not
making much of the forestry certificate, as to whether I get
it or no; but rather, as I should guess, thinking about putting me on this Balnavrain place as soon as it becomes his
own.   Ay, ay, sweetheart; that would be a fine thing for
me, to be in a position just like that of Mr. Crawford—
though on a small scale ; and who could prevent my coming
to claim my good wife then, and declaring her as mine
before all the world?'

'Yes, yes, Ronald,' she said eagerly, 'but why do you
talk like that?   Why do you speak as if there was trouble?
Surely he will make you factor !   It was he that asked you
to go away to Glasgow ; he always was your friend ; if he
buys the estate, who else could he get to manage it as
well ?'

'But there's another thing, sweetheart,' said he, rather hopelessly. 'He spoke about it yesterday. Indeed, he put it plain enough. He asked me fairly whether, supposing somebody was to offer me the management of an estate, I could get guarantees—securities for my honesty, in fact; and he even mentioned the sum that would be needed. Well, well, it's beyond me, my girl—where could I find two people to stand surety for me at £500 apiece?'

She uttered a little cry, and clung closer to him.

'Ronald—Ronald—surely you will not miss such a chance for that—it is a matter of form, isn't it?—and some one——'

'But who do I know that has got £500, and that I could ask?' said he. 'Ay, and two of them. Maybe Lord Ailine might be one—he was always a good friend to me—but two of them—two of them—well, well, good lass, if it has all got to go, we must wait for some other chance.'

'Yes,' said Meenie bitterly, 'and this American—he calls himself a friend of yours too—and he wants guarantees for your honesty!'

'It's the usual thing, as he said himself,' Ronald said. 'But don't be downhearted, my dear. Hopes and disappointments come to every one, and we must meet them like the rest. The world has always something for us—even these few minutes—with your cheeks grown warm again—and the scent of your hair—ay, and your heart as gentle as ever.'

But she was crying a little.

'Ronald—surely—it is not possible this chance should be so near us—and then to be taken away. And can't I do something? I know the Glengask people will be angry —but—but I would write to Lady Stuart—or if I could

only go to her, that would be better—it would be between
woman and woman, and surely she would not refuse when
she knew how we were placed—and—and it would be
something for me to do—for you know you've married a
pauper bride, Ronald—and I bring you nothing—when
even a farmer's daughter would have her store of napery
and a chest of drawers and all that—but couldn't I do this,
Ronald?—I would go and see Lady Stuart—she could
not refuse me!'

He laughed lightly; and his hands were clasped round
the soft brown hair.

'No, no, no, sweetheart; things will have come to a
pretty pass before I would have you exposed to any
humiliation of that sort. And why should you be down-
hearted? The world is young for both of us. Oh, don't
you be afraid; a man that can use his ten fingers and is
willing to work will tumble into something sooner or later;
and what is the use of being lovers if we are not to have
our constancy tried? No, no; you keep a brave heart:
if this chance has to be given up, we'll fall in with another;
and maybe it will be all the more welcome that we have
had to wait a little while for it.'

'A little while, Ronald?' said she.

He strove to cheer her and reassure her still further;
although, indeed, there was not much time for that; for
he had been commanded to dine with Mr. Hodson at half-
past seven; and he knew better than to keep the man who
might possibly be his master waiting for dinner. And
presently Meenie and he were going quietly along the
snow-hushed road; and he bade her good-bye—many and
many times repeated—near the little garden-gate; and
then made his way back to the inn. He had just time to

brush his hair and smarten himself up a bit when the pretty Nelly—who seemed to be a little more friendly and indulgent towards him than in former days—came to say that she had taken the soup into the parlour, and that the gentleman was waiting.

Now Mr. Hodson was an astute person; and he suspected something, and was anxious to know more; but he was not so ill-advised as to begin with direct questions. For one thing, there was still a great deal to be talked over about the Balnavrain estate—which he had almost decided on purchasing; and, amongst other matters, Ronald was asked whether the overseer of such a place would consider £400 a year a sufficient salary, if a plainly and comfortably built house were thrown in; and also whether, in ordinary circumstances, there would be any difficulty about a young fellow obtaining two sureties to be responsible for him. From that it was a long way round to the Doctor's daughter; but Mr. Hodson arrived there in time; for he had brought for her a present from his own daughter; and he seemed inclined to talk in a friendly way about the young lady. And at last he got the whole story. Once started, Ronald spoke frankly enough. He confessed to his day-dreams about one so far superior to him in station; he described his going away to Glasgow; his loneliness and despair there; his falling among evil companions and his drinking; the message of the white heather; his pulling himself up; and Meenie's sudden resolve and heroic self-surrender. The private marriage, too—yes, he heard the whole story from beginning to end; and the more he heard the more his mind was busy; though he was a quiet kind of person, and the recital did not seem to move him in any way whatever.

And yet it may be doubted whether, in all the county of Sutherland, or in all the realm of England, there was any happier man that night than Mr. Josiah Hodson. For here was something entirely after his own heart. His pet hobby was playing the part of a small beneficent Providence; and he had already befriended Ronald, and was greatly interested in him; moreover, had he not promised his daughter, when she lay apparently very near to death, that Ronald should be looked after? But surely he had never looked forward to any such opportunity as this! And then the girl was so pretty—that, also, was something. His heart warmed to the occasion; dinner being over, they drew their chairs towards the big fireplace where the peats were blazing cheerfully; Ronald was bidden to light his pipe; and then the American—in a quiet, indifferent, sententious way, as if he were talking of some quite abstract and unimportant matter—made his proposal.

'Well, now, Ronald,' said he, as he stirred up some of the peats with his foot, 'you seemed to think that £400 a year and a house thrown in was good enough for the overseer of that Balnavrain place. I don't know what your intentions are; but if you like to take that situation, it's yours.'

Ronald looked startled—but only for a moment.

'I thank ye, sir; I thank ye,' he said, with rather a downcast face. 'I will not say I had no suspicion ye were thinking of some such kindness; and I thank ye—most heartily I thank ye. But it's beyond me. I could not get the securities.'

'Well, now, as to that,' the American said, after a moment's consideration, 'I am willing to take one security —I mean for the whole amount; and I want to name the

person myself. If Miss Douglas will go bail for you—or
Mrs. Strang, I suppose I should call her—then there is no
more to be said. Ronald, my good fellow, if the place is
worth your while, take it; it's yours.'

A kind of flash of joy and gratitude leapt to the younger
man's eyes; but all he could manage to say was—

'If I could only tell *her!*'

'Well, now, as to that again,' said Mr. Hodson, rising
slowly, and standing with his back to the fire, 'I have got
to take along that present from my daughter—to-morrow
morning would be best; and I could give her the information, if you wished. But I'll tell you what would be still
better, my friend: you just let me settle this little affair
with the old people—with the mamma, as I understand.
I'm not much of a talkist; but if you give me permission
I'll have a try; I think we might come to some kind of a
reasonable understanding, if she doesn't flatten me with
her swell relations. Why, yes, I think I can talk sense to
her. I don't want to see the girl kept in that position;
your Scotch ways—well, we haven't got any old ballads in
my country, and we like to have our marriages fair and
square and aboveboard: now let me tell the old lady the
whole story, and try to make it up with her. She can't
scold my head off.'

And by this time he was walking up and down the
room; and he continued—

'No; I shall go round to-morrow afternoon, when we
come back from the fishing. And look here, Ronald; this
is what I want you to do; you must get the other boat
down to the lake—and you will go in that one—and get
another lad or two—I will pay them anything they want.
I can't have my overseer acting as gillie, don't you see—if

I am going to talk with his mother-in-law ; you must get
out the other boat ; and if you catch a salmon or two, just
you send them along to the Doctor, with your compliments
—do you hear, your compliments, not mine.   Now——'

'And I have not a word of thanks !' Ronald exclaimed.
'My head is just bewildered——'

'Say, now,' the American continued quietly—in fact, he
seemed to be considering his finger-nails more than anything else, as he walked up and down the room—'say, now,
what do you think the Doctor's income amounts to in the
year ?   Not much ?   Two hundred pounds with all expenses
paid ?'

'I really don't know,' Ronald said—not understanding
the drift of this question.

'Not three hundred, anyway ?'

'I'm sure I don't know.'

'Ah.   Well, now, I've got to talk to that old lady to-
morrow about the prospects of her son-in-law—though she
don't know she has got one,' Mr. Hodson was saying—half
to himself, as it were.   'I suppose she'll jump on me when
I begin.   But there's one thing.   If I can't convince her
with four hundred a year, I'll try her with five—and Carry
shall kiss me the difference.'

CHAPTER XVI.

THE FACTOR OF BALNAVRAIN.

WELL, now, some couple of months or so thereafter, this same Miss Carry was one of a party of four—all Americans —who set out from Lairg station to drive to Inver-Mudal; and very comfortable and content with each other they seemed to be when they were ensconced in the big waggonette. For a convalescent, indeed, Miss Hodson appeared to be in excellent spirits; but there may have been reasons for that; for she had recently become engaged; and her betrothed, to mark that joyful circumstance, had left for Europe with her; and it was his first trip to English shores; and more especially it was his first trip to the Highlands of Scotland; and very proud was she of her self-imposed office of chaperon and expounder and guide. Truth to tell, the long and lank editor found that in many respects he had fallen upon troublous times; for not only was he expected to be profoundly interested in historical matters about which he did not care a red cent, and to accept any and every inconvenience and discomfort as if it were a special blessing from on high, and to be ready at all moments to admire mountains and glens and lakes when he would much rather have been talking of something more personal to Miss Carry and himself, but also—and this was the cruellest wrong of all

—he had to listen to continued praises of Ronald Strang that now and again sounded suspiciously like taunts.   And on such occasions he was puzzled by the very audacity of her eyes.   She regarded him boldly—as if to challenge him to say that she did not mean every word she uttered ; and he dared not quarrel with her, or dispute ; though sometimes he had his own opinion as to whether those pretty soft dark eyes were quite so innocent and simple and straightforward as they pretended to be.

'Ah,' said she, as they were now driving away from the village into the wide, wild moorland, 'ah, when you see Ronald, you will see a man.'

She had her eyes fixed on him.

'I suppose they don't grow that kind of a thing in our country,' he answered meekly.

'I mean,' she said, with a touch of pride, 'I mean a man who is not ashamed to be courteous to women—a man who knows how to show proper respect to women.'

'Why, yes, I'll allow you won't find that quality in an American,' he said, with a subtle sarcasm that escaped her, for she was too obviously bent on mischief.

'And about the apology, now ?'

'What apology ?'

'For your having published an insulting article about Ronald, to be sure.   Of course you will have to apologise to him, before this very day is over.'

'I will do anything else you like,' the long editor said, with much complaisance.   'I will fall in love with the young bride, if you like.   Or I'll tell lies about the weight of the salmon when I get back home.   But an apology ? Seems to me a man making an apology looks about as foolish as a woman throwing a stone : I don't see my way

to that. Besides, where does the need of it come in, anyhow? You never read the article. It was very com-
plimentary, as I think; yes, it was so; a whole column and
more about a Scotch gamekeeper——'

'A Scotch gamekeeper!' Miss Carry said proudly.
'Well, now, just you listen to me. Ronald knows nothing
at all about this article; if he did, he would only laugh at
it; but he never heard of it; and it's not to be spoken of
here. But I mean to speak of it, by and by. I mean to
speak of it, when I make the acquaintance of—what's his
distinguished name?——'

But here Miss Kerfoot—who, with her married sister,
occupied the other side of the waggonette—broke in.

'You two quarrelling again!' And then she sighed.
'But what is the good of a drive, anyway, when we haven't
got Doctor Tom and his banjo?'

'A banjo—in Strath-Terry?' Miss Carry cried. 'Do
you mean to say you would like to hear a banjo tinkle-
tinkling in a country like this?'

'Yes, my dyaw,' said Miss Kerfoot coolly: she had
been making some studies in English pronunciation, and
was getting on pretty well.

'I suppose you can't imagine how Adam passed the
time without one in the Garden of Eden—wanted to play
to Eve on the moonlight nights—a cake-walk, I suppose—
pumpkin-pie—why, I wonder what's the use of bringing
you to Europe.'

For answer Miss Kerfoot began to hum to herself—but
with the words sounding clearly enough—

> *'I'se gwine back to Dixie,*
> *I'se gwine back to Dixie,*
> *I'se gwine where the orange blossoms grow ;*

> *O, I'd rather be in Dixie,*
> *I'd rather be in Dixie,*
> *For travelling in the Highlands is so——'*

But here remorse of conscience smote her; and she seized Carry's hand.

'No, I won't say it—you poor, weak, invalid thing. And were they worrying you about the Highlands, and the slow trains, and the stuffy omnibus at Lairg? Well, they shan't say anything more to you—that they shan't; and you are to have everything your own way; and I'm going to fall in love with Ronald, just to keep you company.'

But alas! when they did eventually get to Inver-Mudal, there was no Ronald to be found there. Mr. Murray was there, and Mrs. Murray, and the yellow-haired Nelly; and the travellers were told that luncheon was awaiting them; and also that Mr. Hodson had had the second boat put in readiness, lest any of them should care to try the fishing in the afternoon.

'But where is Ronald?' said Miss Carry, not in the least concealing her vexation.

'Don't cry, poor thing,' Miss Kerfoot whispered to her. 'It shall have its Ronald!'

'Oh, don't bother!' she said angrily. 'Mr. Murray, where is Ronald? Is he with my father on the loch?'

'No, no; it's the two gillies that's with Mr. Hodson on the loch,' the innkeeper said. 'And do not you know, Miss, that Ronald is not here at ahl now; he is away at the place in Ross-shire.'

'Oh yes, I know that well enough,' she said, 'but my father wrote that he was coming over to see us for a day or two; and he was to be here this morning—and his wife

as well.   But it is of no consequence.   I suppose we had
better go in and have lunch now.'

Miss Kerfoot was covertly laughing.   But there was a
young lad there called Johnnie—a shy lad he was, and he
was standing apart from the others, and thus it was that
he could see along the road leading down to the Mudal
bridge.   Something in that direction attracted Johnnie's
attention ; he came over and said a word or two to Mr.
Murray; the innkeeper went to the gable of the house,
so that he could get a look up Tongue way, and then
he said—

'Oh yes, I think that will be Ronald.'

'Don't you hear?' said Miss Kerfoot, who was following
the others into the inn.   'They say that Ronald is coming
right now.'

Miss Carry turned at once, and went to where the innkeeper was standing.   Away along there, and just coming
over the bridge, was a dog-cart, with two figures in it.
She watched it.   By and by it was pulled up in front of
the Doctor's cottage ; she guessed that that was Meenie
who got down from the vehicle and went into the house ;
no doubt this was Ronald who was now bringing the dog-
cart along to the inn.   And then the others were summoned ; and presently Ronald had arrived and was being
introduced to them ; and Miss Carry had forgotten all her
impatience, for he looked just as handsome and good-
natured and modest-eyed as ever ; and it was very clear
that Miss Kerfoot was much impressed with the frankness
and simplicity of his manner; and the editor strove to be
particularly civil ; and Mrs. Lalor regarded the new-comer
with an obviously approving glance.   For they all had heard
the story ; and they were interested in him, and in his

young wife; besides, they did not wish to wound the feelings of this poor invalid creature—and they knew what she
thought of Ronald.

And how was he to answer all at once these hundred
questions about the Ross-shire place, and the house that
was building for them, and the farm where he and his wife
were temporarily staying?

'Come in and have lunch with us, Ronald,' said Miss
Carry, in her usual frank way, 'and then you will tell us all
about it. We were just going in; and it's on the table.'

'I cannot do that very well, I thank ye,' said he, 'for I
have to go back to the Doctor's as soon as I have seen the
mare looked after——'

'Oh, but I thought you were coming down to the loch
with us!' she said, with very evident disappointment.

'Yes, yes, to be sure!' said he. 'I'll be back in a
quarter of an hour at the furthest; and then I'll take one
of the lads with me and we'll have the other boat got out
as well.'

'But you don't understand, Ronald,' she said quickly.
'The other boat is there—ready—and two gillies, and rods,
and everything. I only want you to come with us for luck;
there's always good luck when you are in the boat. Ah,
do you know what they did to me on Lake George?'

'Indeed, I was sorry to hear of it, Miss,' said he gravely.

'Miss!' she repeated, with a kind of reproach; but she
could not keep the others waiting any longer; and so there
was an appointment made that they were all to meet at the
loch-side in half an hour; and she and her friends went
into the house.

When it came to setting out, however, Mrs. Lalor
begged to be excused; she was a little bit tired, she said,

and would go and lie down. So the other three went by themselves; and when they got down to the loch, they not only found that Ronald was there awaiting them, but also that Mr. Hodson had reeled up his lines and come ashore to welcome them. Of course that was the sole reason. At the same time the gillies had got out three remarkably handsome salmon and put them on the grass; and that was the display that met the eyes of the strangers when they drew near. Mr. Hodson was not proud; but he admitted that they were good-looking fish. Yes; it was a fair morning's work. But there were plenty more where these came from, he said encouragingly; they'd better begin.

Whereupon Miss Carry said promptly—

'Come along, Em. Mr. Huysen, will you go with pappa, when he is ready? And Ronald will come with us, to give us good luck at the start.'

Miss Kerfoot said nothing, but did as she was bid; she merely cast a glance at Mr. Huysen as they were leaving; and her eyes were demure.

However, if she considered this manœuvre—as doubtless she did—a piece of mere wilful and perverse coquetry on the part of her friend, she was entirely mistaken. It simply never would have entered Miss Carry's head that Ronald should have gone into any other person's boat, so long as she was there—nor would it have entered his head either. But besides that, she had brought something for him; and she wished to have time to show it to him; and so, when the boat was well away from the shore, and when he had put out both the lines, she asked him to be so kind as to undo the long case lying there, and to put the rod together, and say what he thought of it. It was a salmon-rod, she explained; of American make; she had heard they were considered rather superior articles; and if he approved of this one, she begged that he would keep it.

He looked up with a little surprise.

'Ye are just too kind,' said he.   'There's that beautiful rug that you sent to my wife, now——'

'But isn't it useful?' she said, in her quick, frank way. 'Isn't it comfortable?   When you were coming along this morning, didn't she find it comfortable?'

'Bless me!' he cried.   'Do you think she would put a beautiful thing like that into a dog-cart to be splashed with mud, and soiled with one's boots?   No, no; it's put over an easy-chair at the Doctor's, until we get a house of our own, and proud she is of it, as she ought to be.'

And proud was he, too, of this beautiful rod—if he declared that it was far too fine for this coarse trolling work; and Miss Kerfoot arrived at the impression that if he could not make pretty speeches of thanks, there was that in his manner that showed he was not ungrateful.

Nor was Miss Carry's faith in Ronald's good luck belied; for they had not been more than twenty minutes out on the loch when they had got hold of something; and at once she rose superior to the excitement of the gillies, and to the consternation of her American friend. Perhaps she was showing off a little; at all events, she seemed quite cool and collected, as if this strain on the rod and the occasional long scream of the reel were a usual kind of thing; and Ronald looked on in quiet composure, believing that his pupil was best left alone.   But alas! alas! for that long illness.   The fish was a heavy one and a game fighter; Miss Carry's arms were weaker than she had thought; at the end of about a quarter of an hour—during which time the salmon had been plunging and boring and springing, and making long rushes in every conceivable manner—she began to feel the strain. But she was a brave lass; as long as ever she could stand upright, she held on; then she said, rather faintly—

'Ronald!'

''Take the rod,' she said, 'the fish isn't played out; but I am.'

'What's the matter?' said he, in great alarm, as she sank on to the seat.

'Oh, nothing, nothing,' she said, though she was a little pale. 'Give Em the rod—give Miss Kerfoot the rod—quick, Em, get up and land your first salmon.'

'Oh my gracious, no! I should die of fright!' was the immediate answer.

But Ronald had no intention of allowing Miss Carry's salmon to be handed over to any one else. He turned to the gillies.

'Is there not a drop of whisky in the boat? Quick, lads, if you have such a thing—quick, quick!—'

They handed him a small green bottle; but she shrank from it.

'The taste is too horrid for anything,' she said. 'But I will have another try. Stand by me, Ronald; and mind I don't fall overboard.'

She got hold of the rod again; he held her right arm—but only to steady her.

'Carry—Carry!' her friend said anxiously. 'I wish you'd leave it alone. Remember, you've been ill—it's too much for you—oh, I wish the thing would go away!'

'I mean to wave the banner over this beast, if I die for it,' Miss Carry said, under her breath; and Ronald laughed —for that was more of his way of thinking.

'We'll have him, sure enough,' he said. 'Ay, and a fine fish, too, that I know.'

'Oh, Ronald!' she cried.

For there was a sudden and helpless slackening of the line. But she had experience enough to reel up hard ; and presently it appeared that the salmon was there—very much there, in fact, for now it began to go through some performances—within five-and-twenty yards of the boat— that nearly frightened Miss Kerfoot out of her wits. And then these cantrips moderated slowly down ; the line was got in shorter ; Ronald, still steadying Miss Carry's right arm with his left hand, got hold of the clip in the other ; and the young lady who was the spectator of all this manœuvring began rather to draw away in fear, as that large white gleaming thing showed nearer and nearer the coble. Nay, she uttered a quick cry of alarm when a sudden dive of the steel hook brought out of the water a huge silvery creature that the next moment was in the bottom of the boat ; and then she found that Carry had sunk down beside her, pretty well exhausted, but immensely proud ; and that the gillies were laughing and vociferous and excited over the capture ; and Ronald calmly getting out his scale-weight from his pocket. The other boat was just then passing.

'A good one?' Mr. Hodson called out.

'Just over sixteen pounds, sir.'

'Well done. But leave us one or two ; don't take them all.'

Miss Carry paid no heed. She was far too much exhausted ; but pleased and satisfied, also, that she had been able to see this fight to the end. And she remembered enough of the customs of the country to ask the two gillies

to take a dram—though it had to come from their own
bottle; she said she would see that that was replenished
when they got back to the inn.

It was a beautiful clear evening as they all of them—
the fishing having been given up for the day—walked away
through the meadows, and up into the road, and so on to
the little hamlet; the western sky was shining in silver-gray
and lemon and saffron; and there was a soft sweet feeling
almost as of summer in the air, though the year was yet
young. They had got six fish all told; that is to say, Mr.
Hodson's boat had got one more in the afternoon; while
Miss Carry had managed to pick up a small thing of eight
pounds or so just as they were leaving off. The fact was,
they did not care to prosecute the fishing till the last
moment; for there was to be a little kind of a dinner-
celebration that evening; and no doubt some of them
wanted to make themselves as smart as possible—though
the possibilities, as a rule, don't go very far in the case of
a fishing-party in a Highland inn—all to pay due honour
to the bride.

And surely if ever Meenie could lay claim to the title
of Rose-Meenie it was on this evening when she came
among these stranger folk—who were aware of her story,
if not a word was said or hinted of it—and found all the
women be-petting her. And Mrs. Douglas was there,
radiant in silk and ribbons, if somewhat austere in manner;
and the big good-natured Doctor was there, full to over-
flowing with jests and quips and occult Scotch stories; and
Mr. and Mrs. Murray had done their very best for the
decoration of the dining-room—though Sutherlandshire in
April is far from being Florida. And perhaps, too, Miss
Carry was a little paid out when she saw the perfectly

servile adulation which Mr. J. C. Huysen (who had a sensitive heart, according to the young men of the *N. Y. Sun*) laid at the feet of the pretty young bride ; though Mr. Hodson rather interfered with that, claiming Mrs. Strang as his own.   Of course, Miss Kerfoot was rather downhearted, because of the absence of her Tom and his banjo ; but Ronald had promised her she should kill a salmon on the morrow ; and that comforted her a little.   Mrs. Lalor had recovered, and was chiefly an amused spectator ; there was a good deal of human nature about ; and she had eyes.

Altogether it was a pleasant enough evening ; for, although the Americans and the Scotch are the two nations out of all the world that are the most madly given to after-dinner speech-making, nothing of the kind was attempted : Mr. Hodson merely raised his glass and gave 'The Bride !' and Ronald said a few manly and sensible words in reply. Even Mrs. Douglas so far forgot the majesty of Glengask and Orosay as to become quite complaisant ; perhaps she reflected that it was, after all, chiefly through the kindness of these people that her daughter and her daughter's husband had been placed in a comfortable and assured position.

Ronald and Meenie had scarcely had time as yet to cease from being lovers ; and so it was that on this same night he presented her with two or three more of those rhymes that sometimes he still wrote about her when the fancy seized him.   In fact, he had written these verses as he sate on the deck of the big screw-steamer, when she was slowly steaming up the Raasay Sound.

> *O what's the sweetest thing there is*
> *In all the wide, wide world ?—*

A rose that hides its deepest scent
  In the petals closely curled?

Or the honey that's in the clover;
  Or the lark's song in the morn;
Or the wind that blows in summer
  Across the fields of corn;

Or the dew that the queen of the fairies
  From her acorn-chalice sips?
Ah no: for sweeter and sweeter far
  Is a kiss from Meenie's lips!

And Meenie was pleased—perhaps, indeed, she said as much and showed as much, when nobody was by; but all the same she hid away the little fragment among a mass of similar secret treasures she possessed; for she was a young wife now; and fully conscious of the responsibilities of her position; and well was she aware that it would never do for any one to imagine that nonsense of that kind was allowed to interfere with the important public duties of the factor of Balnavrain.

THE END.

A Selection from Macmillan's Popular Novels.

In Crown 8vo, cloth. Price 6s. each Volume.

By CHARLES KINGSLEY.

Westward Ho!
Hereward the Wake.
Two Years Ago.
Alton Locke. With Portrait.
Yeast. | Hypatia.

John Inglesant. By J. H. SHORT-HOUSE.
Tom Brown's Schooldays.
Tom Brown at Oxford.
A Family Affair. By HUGH CONWAY.
Bengal Peasant Life. By LAL BEHARI DAY.
Virgin Soil. By TOURGÉNIEF.
Miss Bretherton. By Mrs. HUMPHRY WARD.
Bethesda. By BARBARA ELBON.
Jill. By E. A. DILLWYN.
Mitchelhurst Place. By MARGARET VELEY.

By THE AUTHOR OF "JOHN HALIFAX, GENTLEMAN."

The Ogilvies. Illustrated by J. M. M'RALSTON.
The Head of the Family. Illustrated by WALTER CRANE.
Olive. Illustrated by G. BOWERS.
Agatha's Husband. Illustrated by WALTER CRANE.
My Mother and I. Illustrated by J. M. M'RALSTON.
Miss Tommy. Illustrated by F. NOËL PATON.

By CHARLOTTE M. YONGE.

The Heir of Redclyffe.
Heartsease.
Hopes and Fears.
The Daisy Chain.
Pillars of the House. 2 vols.
The Clever Woman of the Family.
Dynevor Terrace.
The Young Stepmother.

By CHARLOTTE M. YONGE—
Continued.

The Trial.
My Young Alcides.
The Three Brides.
The Caged Lion.
The Dove in the Eagle's Nest.
Love and Life.
The Chaplet of Pearls.
Lady Hester and the Danvers Papers.
Magnum Bonum.
Unknown to History.
Stray Pearls.
The Armourer's 'Prentices.

By ANNIE KEARY.

Castle Daly.
A Doubting Heart.
Oldbury.
A York and a Lancaster Rose.
Clemency Franklyn.

By HENRY JAMES.

The American.
The Europeans.
Daisy Miller: An International Episode: Four Meetings.
Roderick Hudson.
The Madonna of the Future, and other Tales.
Washington Square: The Pension Beaurepas: A Bundle of Letters.
The Portrait of a Lady.
Stories Revived. Two Series.

By FRANCIS H. BURNETT.

Haworth's.
Louisiana; and That Lass o' Lowrie's.

By MRS. OLIPHANT.

Hester.
Sir Tom.
The Wizard's Son.
A Beleaguered City.

MACMILLAN AND CO., LONDON.